Ravenhall

By Peter McFarlane

Note for Librarians: A cataloguing record for this book is available from Library and Archives Canada at www.collectionscanada.ca/amicus/index-e.html
ISBN 1-4120-5537-7

Printed on paper with minimum 30% recycled fibre.
Trafford's print shop runs on "green energy" from solar, wind and other environmentally-friendly power sources.

TRAFFORD PUBLISHING™

Offices in Canada, USA, Ireland and UK
This book was published on-demand in cooperation with Trafford Publishing. On-demand publishing is a unique process and service of making a book available for retail sale to the public taking advantage of on-demand manufacturing and Internet marketing. On-demand publishing includes promotions, retail sales, manufacturing, order fulfilment, accounting and collecting royalties on behalf of the author.

Book sales for North America and international:
Trafford Publishing, 6E–2333 Government St.,
Victoria, BC V8T 4P4 CANADA
phone 250 383 6864 (toll-free 1 888 232 4444)
fax 250 383 6804; email to orders@trafford.com
Book sales in Europe:
Trafford Publishing (UK) Limited, 9 Park End Street, 2nd Floor
Oxford, UK OX1 1HH UNITED KINGDOM
phone 44 (0)1865 722 113 (local rate 0845 230 9601)
facsimile 44 (0)1865 722 868; info.uk@trafford.com
Order online at:
trafford.com/05-0435

10 9 8 7 6 5 4 3 2

This book is dedicated to Laura, Jack, and Ani.

My three beautiful children.

And to Claire, my wife, for continued support and encouragement.

No matter what life; has thrown our way. x

Chapter 1

THE THREE COMPANIONS

Finn Blackwell awoke as the sun crept into his bedroom. He glanced around, his TV was still on from the night before, a glass of pop spilt on the floor next to his bed. His eyes became fixed on his calendar; a huge grin spread across his face, almost splitting it in two.

"Finn! Finn!" it was Erin, Finn's twin sister. "Are you awake?" Erin came rushing into Finn's room, her excitement uncontrollable. She didn't even notice the sticky pool of pop she was now standing barefoot in. "It's our holidays, get up! We're going to Ping."

Ping is a small hamlet on the rugged north-western coast of Scotland, a favourite holiday destination of Mr and Mrs Blackwell, but one which they had not visited for some time.

Finn sprang out of bed, washed, dressed and raced downstairs, Erin close behind him.

"Come on you two, breakfast is ready. Porridge; just to get us in the mood." Mrs Blackwell placed a bowl of white; lumpy; porridge in front of each of them. Erin and Finn looked at each other.

"Come on, eat up! A traditional Scottish breakfast to get us going, we have a long drive ahead."

Thirty minutes later the car was packed, Mr and Mrs Blackwell in the front, Finn and Erin in the back. Mr Blackwell turned the key in the ignition and the car fired into life; he reversed into the road outside their house, beeped the horn and they were off.

The trip was long and tiring for Mr and Mrs Blackwell, and long and boring for Erin and Finn. Sightseeing came rather low on the list of things that they liked to do.

It was 8pm as they drove into the sleepy little hamlet of Ping. It was cold, dark and raining; the way was dimly lit, by just a couple of street lights. Ping was not a very modern place—by anyone's standards.

"It should be along here," Mr Blackwell yawned.

They were looking for number thirteen; number thirteen Thistle Lane, Ping, Scotland.

"It's there, I see it!" shouted Erin. Sure enough there it was.

The Eagle View Guest House, Thirteen Thistle Lane, Ping. Mr Blackwell parked the car and they all dashed, through the rain, to the door of the guesthouse.

****

Mrs Blackwell rang the bell and they waited. Eventually, after what seemed like a lifetime to Erin and Finn, the large (and rather imposing) wooden door creaked open. Finn held his breath; Erin stood motionless, eyes fixed ahead, on the frail old woman, dressed entirely in black, who stood before them.

"Hello," said Mr Blackwell, "we have a booking, two rooms under the name of Blackwell."

The frail old woman, with wiry grey hair and a pale complexion, started to smile, "Och! Of course you have, come into the warmth; it's a wee bit drizzly out there tonight." This was Mrs Mac, proprietor of the Eagle view Guest House for over forty years and never once having set foot outside of Scotland.

"Come and dry yourselves by the fire, then I'll show you to your rooms."

Mrs Mac led them into a huge living room with solid oak panelling and a raging fire which was so big it almost filled an entire wall. Finn and Erin gazed around the room. The walls were covered with old paintings, swords, and even a stag's head, mounted on a large wooden shield.

Eventually Finn's gaze landed on what was probably the largest picture in the room, "where's that?" he asked Mrs Mac.

"Why that's Ping Castle, just half a mile up the road. Deserted now though, hasn't been lived in for over a hundred years. The locals here call it 'The Dark Castle,' not a place for youngsters to visit." With that, Mrs Mac rushed out of the living room.

"This way to your rooms," she cheerily announced, as she led them up a sweeping staircase.

"Rooms seven and seven and a half, round the corner on the left. Come on, hurry along."

Finn and Erin looked at each other; '*seven and a half*!' what a strange room number they both thought. Their room was softly lit by a small lamp which sat on a large dresser. The mirror reflected the lamp's light and cast shadows on the wall opposite. The beds were comfortable and it was not long before Finn and Erin were asleep; lost in dreams of castles, monsters... and porridge!!!

****

They awoke, early the next morning, to the most mouth-watering aromas they had ever smelled. Soon they were sitting in the dining room, being served the most enormous plateful; of bacon, Lorne sausage, black pudding and fried eggs. The dining room was a bustling hive of activity, with several other guests happily tucking into their breakfasts. Through the kitchen door Finn caught a glimpse of Mrs Mac, dashing around the kitchen, organising her staff with military precision. Soon they were fed, watered and ready to explore.

"Don't go too far," said Mrs Blackwell as Finn and Erin left the Eagle View guesthouse. They set off along Thistle Lane, in the direction of Ping Castle.

"There it is."

Erin had spotted Ping castle at the end of the lane. It was a grey-looking building, with stone walls and turrets which reached high into the clear blue sky. It nestled, silently, in the distance, surrounded by overgrown trees and shrubs. As they got closer, the trees and shrubs got thicker; brambles and nettles erupted everywhere. Finn yelped aloud as the thorns wrapped themselves around his feet and the nettles stung and nipped at his legs. A few moments later, they stood in front of an enormous metal gate, rusted with age and neglect. Fixed to the gate was a dirty old sign, on which only a few words could easily be made out.

"Trespass! Death! I don't like the sound of that," said Erin, wiping the rest of the sign with her sleeve to expose the full (and foreboding) message:

Ping Castle.
Closed To Public Access
By Order Of
Sir Theodore Ping, Laird of This Land
Trespassers Enter At Risk Of:
Disembowelment, Mutilation and Death.

"That's it," said Erin. "Disembowelment! I'm not going another foot closer. I'm happy with my body parts and I intend keeping them." Finn just laughed; and before Erin had time to say 'disembowelment' one more time, he had squeezed through the rusted gate and was heading towards the castle.

"Come on," he shouted, "don't believe what that stupid sign says! I've never heard anything so silly in all my life."

Erin took a deep breath and reluctantly followed Finn into the castle grounds.

Her heart raced as she tried to catch up with Finn—and she felt strangely hot and cold at the same time.

"Finn, wait for me."

Erin sensed something was not right. She felt as if a thousand eyes were staring at her and she could hear a hooting noise overhead. She froze, not daring to move an inch. She tried to call out to Finn once more, but the words would not leave her mouth. Standing directly in front of her was a huge, monster of a man. He must have been seven feet tall and was wrapped in what looked like it was once a wild animal. His face, or indeed what could be seen of it, was all red and blotchy. On his head, he had a striking mass of orange hair; and a beard, so bushy, it could have been home to a dozen hamsters. He wore a red tartan kilt, complete with sporran. A matching length of red tartan draped over his shoulder and tied around his waist. On his feet he wore the biggest pair of boots that Erin had ever seen. Her voice returned. She began to scream uncontrollably. Turning to run, she snagged her foot in a knot of shrubs and roots which made her fall forwards, striking her head on the trunk of a tree. Everything started to slow down from that point, her world began to spin and her hearing became muffled. Erin felt that she was surely dying, as her body had started to lift off the ground, as if being drawn up to heaven. At that point she passed out and could remember no more.

Finn stopped dead in his tracks, sensing something was wrong. It was a strange feeling, one that he had sensed many times before—whenever Erin hurt herself or felt threatened—a 'twin thing,' they would always say.

He stood motionless for a moment as a blinding pain shot through his right temple. He turned, now knowing something was wrong. He quickly started to retrace his steps. He could now see this huge, hulk of a man walking towards him, carrying what looked like some sort of dead animal. As the man approached, Finn could see that he wasn't carrying a dead animal at all—it was Erin.

"Hey you!" shouted Finn as he started running towards them. "What have you done to my sister? What have you done?"

"Calm down laddie, I've dun nothing to yer sister, she's tumbled and banged her heed."

"Who are you?" demanded Finn.

"Why, I'm Willie... Willie McDougal, gamekeeper of these lands... and you're trespassing! Come on, follow me. We have to see to yer sister's heed."

Finn followed Willie as he carried Erin, along a wooded path. Soon they came upon an opening in the trees, where stood a small, stone, cottage.

"Hame at last," roared Willie, "ma wee lodge." Willie kicked open the wooden door and stepped inside. "Come on laddie, follow me in, I'll no bite ye."

Finn followed inside. Willie placed Erin on a settee, big enough for an entire football team, next to a large, crackling, open fire. Willie went to the kitchen and came back with a damp towel, which he carefully placed on Erin's forehead.

"That should do the trick. We locals believe the burn water has magical healing powers."

Erin slept for most of the day, the bang on her head had knocked her for six! Then, slowly, she started to come round. She murmured to herself for a while before opening her eyes.

"Am I in heaven?" she asked, glancing around the room.

Finn sat in a large armchair, a beaming smile on his face.

"Did you die too?" she continued.

"Don't be silly," replied Finn, "we're not dead, we're in the lodge house; the lodge house of Ping Castle."

"But I remember falling, then floating—upwards—towards heaven!"

Willie stepped from the kitchen into the room. "I know I'm tall, but I dinna think I could lift you quite that far lassie. I just picked ye up from where ye fell."

Erin started to whimper, "It's a giant."

"Don't worry that's no giant, that's Willie, Ping Castle's gamekeeper," said Finn, reassuringly.

"And who might *you* be?" asked Willie, in a much mellower tone.

"Er- Erin Blackwell sir; and that's my twin brother, Finn."

"*Mmm*," thought Willie. "And pray tell, what might Erin and Finn Blackwell be doing, trespassing on Sir Theodore Ping's property? Did ye no see the sign?"

Finn and Erin nodded together. "Are you going to disembowel us?" whispered Erin, her voice trembling.

Willie grinned, "Nae lassie, disembowelment is nae my thing.... anyway where are ye folks?"

"The Eagle View guest house," piped up Finn. "We're on our holidays."

"The Eagle View eh? Well you'll no be going back there tonight. Dangerous place these woods at night! I'll give Mrs Mac a ring and let her know where ye are, she'll tell ye parents; stop em worrying."

Willie made a phone call to Mrs Mac. "Aye Mrs Mac both young un's are here," he said.

"That's a relief, their folks were just starting to worry. I'll let them know that they're both safe, and sound, and with you till morning," replied Mrs Mac.

"Best not venture out tonight, there's a storm brewing. Any problems and I'll ring you right back Willie," she continued.

Willie placed the phone on the receiver, as Finn and Erin huddled together on his settee. "Aye, get comfy, you'll sleep here tonight." Willie threw another log on his fire, which roared with delight, the flames flickering and dancing in the middle of the room.

Just as Erin and Finn were starting to relax in Willie's company, the door of the lodge flew open and in stepped a young boy. A very strange-looking young boy, no more than thirteen years old, but already, with a mass of orange hair. He was dressed in a green tartan shirt, which was almost popping open as his belly strained to get out. He wore dark trousers, held up with a piece of string; and a pair of leather boots,—just like Willie's,—only not quite as big.

"Ahh, Cameron son, where have ye bin? I was getting worried!"

"I told ye father, I've bin mushing."

Cameron was Willie's son and it didn't need a lot of common sense to see that. Spitting image—apart from the beard of course.

"Cameron, I'd like ye to meet oor guests; Erin and Finn. They'll be staying the night with us."

Cameron walked across to where Erin and Finn were sitting. "Pleased to meet ye. Are ye hungry? I'm a'ways hungry!" Cameron smiled, his chubby cheeks lifted upwards, almost popping his eyes out of his head.

"Starving!" replied Finn.

With that, Cameron passed a huge box to Willie. "Father makes the best mushie omelette in Scotland!"

"Mushies? what are mushies?" asked Erin.

"Why, mushrooms of course! The biggest, juiciest mushrooms in the whole of Scotland—and they grow right here. Green uns, yellow uns—even purple uns!"

"Purple?" exclaimed Erin.

"Aye, they grow wild right here, just next to the castle."

It wasn't long before the sweetest, most mouth watering, smell of mushroom omelette came wafting from the kitchen. "There ye go," said Willie, as he produced the largest omelette Erin and Finn had ever seen. "Tuck in, plenty to go round."

With that, Finn, Erin, Cameron and Willie, all started to eat. The lovely, buttery, omelette filled them fit to bursting.

"Well what did you think? Aren't they the best mushies you've ever tasted?"

Erin and Finn, mouths still full, nodded in agreement.

After they had all finished eating, the three youngsters—and Willie—settled down in front of the fire.

"Tell us a story father," asked Cameron.

"Alright then, let me see." Willie scratched his head.

"Tell us about Ping Castle," begged Finn.

"You mean, 'The Dark Castle,' as *we* call it," replied Willie. "Well, where to begin.? The castle has been neglected now for about a hundred years, ever since Laird Theodore disappeared. Funny goings-on that night, or so they say. See, Laird Theodore was said to be meddling with strange magic stuff—and the afterlife."

"The what?" asked Erin, obviously, shocked.

"The afterlife. Ye ken, what happens when ye die."

Erin's heart missed a beat at the mere thought of death.

"They do say that if you die within the castle, or its grounds, the secret of its past and the whereabouts of its treasures will be revealed to ye."

"TREASURE!" Finn's eyes lit up.

"Aye laddie, treasure! But, more importantly now, The Purple Crystal of Ping. 'Tis said that it was Laird Theodore's meddling, that plunged the castle into darkness; where no human being would ever set foot again,—if they wanted to continue living, that is."

A shiver ran down Erin's back. "Continue living!"

"All right, that's enough let's change the subject," said Willie.

"But the crystal, where is it?" asked Finn, not wanting the story to end.

"Well, they say it's in the castle somewhere. But no one who has ever gone in has been seen again. A curse—or so it seems." Willie frowned as he spoke, his eyes looked tired? Willie had looked after the Ping Castle Estate all his life, working the land and living off the fruits it bore. Just like his family had always done—even after the castle had fallen into darkness.

"Time to sleep now young uns. And don't be worrying ye'sells yer quite safe here with me," said Willie, smiling reassuringly.

Finn, Erin and Cameron settled into the huge settee, whilst Willie sank into his favourite armchair. It wasn't long before all four were asleep. Even the fire looked tired as it slowly burnt down, giving off just enough light to cast a few shadows across the room.

Finn awoke with a jump, at the sound of rain, beating down on the Ballahulish slate roof. It was rain like he had never heard before. It sounded like hailstones bearing down on them, with such intensity that they bounced and danced around on the roof. The rain got louder and louder, it wasn't long before everyone was awake in the lodge.

"Don't worry it's only the Scottish rain come to say hello," said Willie, trying to reassure them all.

But Cameron was unsure, this was unlike any Scottish rain that he had ever heard before.

Willie could see the worry in his son's face. "Calm yourself Cameron it will soon be...."

Before Willie had chance to finish his sentence there was an almighty flash of lightning, which lit not only the lodge, but probably the whole of Ping. It was as if daylight had just broken. The flash of lightning was quickly followed by a deafening boom, which sounded like a hundred trees being ripped from their roots. Then, silence; even the rain stopped.

The three young companions huddled together on the settee.

"Just a storm. All finished now." Willie forced a smile as he laid a thick blanket over them. "Sleep now, it'll soon be morning."

Willie settled back into his armchair, knowing something was wrong—but what exactly, he didn't know. He drifted in and out of sleep for the rest of the night, one eye open at all times.

Erin was first to awake the next morning. The sun seeped through the windows of the lodge, but it did not bring any warmth, just light.

It wasn't long before all four were awake and Willie was busy, preparing a breakfast of tattie scones and porridge, whilst the three friends chatted excitedly about the storm.

Breakfast was served. "I didn't think porridge could taste so good!" said Finn as he shovelled the stuff in. "Better than mum's any day."

"Right young uns, time to get back to The Eagle View," said Willie.

"Oh! Can't we stay a little longer? It's still early," pleaded Finn.

"Please father, just a bit longer?" begged Cameron.

"Well I suppose; just a bit mind," said Willie looking at a large wooden clock hung on the wall, "I'll contact Mrs Mac, let her know, so she can tell ye parents."

The three friends jumped about excitedly. "This way," said Cameron, "I'll show you where the mushies grow."

"Don't go too far," shouted Willie, as all three ran out of the lodge and into the forest.

Chapter 2

THE BLACK HAMMER

The three friends laughed and played as they ran into the forest. The rain from the previous night had left its mark. The grass was wet and muddy and a sweet, sticky, smell lingered in the air as the wild flowers and heathers gave off their scent.

The closer they got to the castle, the darker it seemed to get.

A cold wind began to blow, sending a shiver down Erin's back, the hairs on the back of her neck stood to attention.

"Wait a moment," she shouted to the boys as she stood still. Her heart began racing and, once more, she sensed a thousand eyes staring at her from within the forest. It was the same feeling she had felt when entering the forest for the first time.

From nowhere, a large bird swooped down on her. It was the size of an owl, but more closely resembled a raven; completely black, with piercing yellow eyes and a hooked beak. Erin felt it brush through her hair. Its claws catching her forehead, drawing blood. She fell to the ground, just as Cameron and Finn reached her side.

"Erin, are you ok?" asked Cameron.

"What was that?" asked Finn, pointing skyward as the bird flew over the castle and out of sight.

"I don't believe it, it can't have been," said Cameron in disbelief.

"What?" asked Finn.

"A Black Hammer; I'm sure it was a Black Hammer!"

Erin, assisted by Cameron, stood to her feet. She wiped the blood from her forehead with her sleeve, thankfully it was just a scratch.

"What's a Black Hammer?" she asked.

"It's a... it's a..." Cameron stuttered as he spoke, still in disbelief at what he thought he had just seen. "It's a keeper of souls. I've never seen one before, but I've heard plenty of stories about them...They say that when you pass to the afterlife, the Black Hammers try to steal your soul, to feed to the most powerful source of evil known to man!"

Finn gasped for breath and his throat tightened, feeling as if he was being starved of oxygen. It felt as though invisible hands were being clasped around his neck, willing the life out of his body. He tried to fight off whatever was attacking him, but to no avail.

He fell to the ground, unconscious.

"Finn, Finn, wake up." Finn could hear Erin's muffled voice calling him, her voice becoming clearer as he started to come round. Opening his eyes he saw Erin and Cameron knelt at his side. "What happened?" he asked, still somewhat dazed and confused.

"You passed out. One minute I was telling you about the Black Hammer, the next you were on the ground. You've been out cold for ages."

"I've seen it," said Finn, still in a state of confusion.

"Seen what?" asked Erin, rather puzzled with the whole situation.

"What Cameron was telling us about, the most powerful source of evil known to man!"

"What?" shrieked Erin, "but there was no one here."

Finn started to nod, "yes there was. He was trying to strangle me. I could feel his hands around my throat. A man—I think he was a man—shrouded in black; his head, covered with a hood...I saw his eyes, piercing yellow, full of evil, just like the Black Hammer."

Erin started to laugh, "are you sure you didn't bang your head when you fell?"

"He's telling the truth. I've heard the stories. The Black Hammer, The Dark Spirit, I've heard them all."

Cameron looked pale as he helped Finn to his feet.

"Yes that's it, that's what he was saying. He told me The Dark Spirit had come for my soul. That's what he whispered as he tried to squeeze the life from me. I remember grabbing at him, trying to fight him off, grabbing at the purple stone he wore around his neck... and then, then he was gone."

Cameron's jaw dropped open as he listened to Finn.

"The Purple Crystal of Ping! He was wearing The Purple Crystal of Ping! It saved your life as you touched it."

The three friends hugged each other, relieved that they were still together and safe, for now.

Cameron and Erin helped Finn back to the lodge. They walked quickly and silently, their senses alert at all times. They scanned the sky for the returning Black Hammer, fearing another attack.

It wasn't long before the lodge came into sight. Willie was standing in the doorway, he could see something was wrong and rushed over to meet them.

"Come on young uns, back in the lodge," said Willie, as he lifted Finn and carried him the rest of the way. "Get by the fire and warm yourselves, I've got a pot of nettle and damson tea on the stove, that should put the colour back in yer cheeks." Willie poured four steaming mugs of tea and handed them around. "Drink up; made with burn water, you'll feel a lot better after you've drunk it."

Cameron, Finn and Erin, sipped at the hot tea; it warmed and calmed them as it trickled into their bellies, their sense of wellbeing returning.

"Father, we saw a Black Hammer in the forest," whispered Cameron, not wanting to distress Erin any further.

"I know son, I saw it too, just after you left the lodge. It flew overhead in the direction of the castle."

"But father, it attacked Erin, grazing her forehead, and then The...The Dark Spirit, it tried to take Finn." Cameron's voice trembled as he raced to get the words out of his mouth.

"Calm yourself son. Whatever it was has gone now."

Willie knew what was happening, but could not quite believe it. Over the years he had been told many stories, by his father and his grandfather. Stories of The Dark Spirit. The Dark Spirit that had taken Ping Castle as its fortress. Stealing and feeding from the souls of departed spirits. Thriving in darkness, increasing in power—until strong enough to be known as the most powerful source of evil known to man. The Dark Spirit would then unleash his power over the face of the world, crushing everything—and everyone—that stood in his path, in his quest for dominance. Willie knew that time was close. The stories that had entertained him as a child and the ones he told his own son, were now coming true.

Willie also knew, if the stories were to be believed, that the only way to destroy The Dark Spirit, was to part him from the Purple Crystal. The very same Purple Crystal the spirit wore around its neck, protecting it from all others. Willie's heart sank. To accomplish such a task would be almost impossible. His eyes closed as he sat back into his armchair to finish his mug of nettle and damson tea.

****

"Right you two, let's get ye back to The Eagle View, back to yer parents. You wait here son, I'll not be long."

Finn and Erin said their goodbyes to Cameron and then left the lodge, setting off in the direction of The Eagle View. As they walked into the small hamlet, Willie noticed how quiet it seemed; the silence was really quite eerie.

They stopped at the local butcher's shop, as Willie fancied some of his favourite haggis for supper. The shop window displayed; an impressive array of local meats, haggis and sloop—a type of pate, made only in Ping.

"Hello... Hamish are ye there?" Willie shouted for the butcher, but there was no one around. In fact, there wasn't anybody anywhere. They walked on until they reached The Eagle View; Willie clenched his fist and hammered on the door.

"Hello Mrs Mac, are ye there? Hello? Mrs Mac?" There was no answer. Willie pushed open the door and stepped inside.

"Hello Mrs Mac, are ye here?" Again silence.

Finn and Erin rushed up to their rooms, they were empty. In fact, the whole of the house was empty.

"Willie, what's happening? Our parents aren't here!" Erin's eyes welled with tears as she frantically looked to Willie for answers.

He wrapped his strong arms around her. "Don't worry lassie, yer parents will be back soon."

Finn just stood, dumbstruck by the situation. He knew what was happening. "The stories about the castle, and The Dark Spirit, they aren't just stories are they?"

Willie stared into Finn's eyes, his frustration and sadness obvious.

"No lad, appears not."

Willie led Erin and Finn out of the Eagle View and back up the road, towards the safety of the lodge.

Cameron rushed out to meet them. "You're back, you're back," he shouted excitedly, unaware of the reason for their swift return.

The three friends sat together in front of the fire. Finn explained the recent events, at the Eagle View and the butcher's shop, to Cameron.

Willie was in the kitchen banging, and clattering. He had a large pot simmering on the stove and was placing things into an old, webbing, sack.

"What are you doing father?" asked Cameron.

Willie did not answer, instead he just continued his work. He took the simmering pan and poured some of its contents into two small glass phials, putting the rest to one side.

"What's that?" asked Finn, inquisitively.

"Pixie Pogrom," replied Willie.

"Pixie what?" asked Cameron.

"Pogrom! Made with magical burn water it is, destroys anything it touches." Willie continued filling his sack.

When he was finished, he walked across to Cameron, Finn and Erin, and sat down.

"Right you three, listen to me. I have to go. There's only one way to end this, I must get the Purple Crystal."

"But father, that's impossible! To get the Crystal you would have to destroy The Dark Spirit," said Cameron, trying to hide his concern.

"No son, not impossible—but not easy either." Willie smiled, trying to make light of the situation, but knowing deep down that if he made one mistake The Dark Spirit would claim his soul.

"I want you three to stay here until I get back. Lock the door behind me and under no circumstances leave the lodge, do you understand?"

The three friends looked at each other, nodding their heads.

Willie made his way to the door, he looked at Cameron.

"I'll be back laddie, have no doubt about that." He opened the door and was gone.

The three friends sat silently for a while, almost in disbelief. Could this really be happening? Could The Dark Spirit really exist—or was this just a nightmare from which they had yet to awake?

The mark on Erin's forehead, from where the Black Hammer had struck, was real enough; so too was the knotted feeling in the pits of their stomachs.

"What do we do now?" asked Erin, hoping the response would resolve her fear.

"We go get the Purple Crystal," said Cameron, determination etched in his expression.

"But Willie told us to stay here until he returned, what if he comes back and we're gone?"

"Cameron is right," interrupted Finn. "We must go and help to get the Crystal. If Willie doesn't return it will be up to us anyway."

The three friends looked at each other for assurance. Cameron stretched out his hands to Erin and Finn. Finn took hold and gripped tightly. Erin didn't move; the boys looked at her, Finn also offering her his hand. The fear in Erin's face was visible to all. *"What to do? what to do?"* she thought. She certainly wasn't going to stay in the lodge on her own. Erin finally grabbed the boys hands.

"Don't be afraid," said Cameron, "I'll protect you."

Erin was reassured by Cameron's kind words, she knew he meant them.

****

"Right, we need to take some things with us," said Cameron. Grabbing an old, cloth rucksack, he carefully placed a handful of rocks from the fireside, into it, along with the catapult he used for hunting rabbits; then an old rope and a glass jar, full of mints.

Erin went to the kitchen and took some food from the larder. Bread, cheese and half a pot of sloop. She wrapped everything carefully in a cloth and placed them into the rucksack.

"Cameron," called Finn excitedly, "theres some Pixie Pogrom left in the pan."

"Careful, don't spill it." Cameron took two small glass phials from under the sink and carefully poured the Pixie Pogrom into them. Not daring to spill a drop, he secured the lids and placed them into his rucksack.

Finn filled a flask with nettle and damson tea, dividing the rest equally into three mugs.

"Drink up, this will give us a boost before we go." Finn handed the drinks round and then all three sat in front of the fire, their minds spinning at the thought of what might be in store for them.

"Where do we go first? How do we get into the castle? What if we can't get back? What if...?"

Cameron placed his arm around Erin, "I know the way in. If we stick together we'll be fine. Just focus on getting the Crystal."

Finn finished his tea and stood up. "I don't quite know how, but we must help Willie. I'm ready to go!"

With that, Cameron and Erin drank the remains of their tea and stood to their feet. All three then left the lodge, setting off through the forest.

****

A cold wind started to blow as Cameron led them towards the castle. Dusk was descending; the rain from the previous night had brought the midges out, swarming under the large oak trees.

"Keep your mouths shut," warned Cameron as he forged ahead, thoughts of his father in his head.

It wasn't long until they came across a fork in the path. "Funny!" exclaimed Cameron, "never seen this before!"

"Are we lost? Do you know where we are going?" asked Erin worriedly.

"Of course we're not lost....it's," Cameron paused momentarily,

"It's this way, follow me."

With that, Cameron led Finn and Erin down the right hand fork in the path.

Soon the pathway became rugged, the shrubs and trees becoming more and more dense.

"Argh!" Shouted Finn, catching his foot in a vine of wild tangle weed—a rope-like shrub, native to Scotland. The tangle weed wound itself around Finn's ankle.

"I'm caught!" he shouted, as the tangle weed got tighter and tighter, its grip almost stopping the circulation to his foot, "it's got me, help!"

Cameron knew straight away what to do. He took a knife from down his sock, traced the tangle weed back to its roots, then with one swift blow, severed the vine. The tangle weed went limp, releasing its grip, it fell away from Finn's ankle.

Erin glanced upwards. "Look! The castle is just ahead."

Cameron smiled to himself, he knew he was heading the right way.

Finn, now free from the tangle weed, stood back up and the three friends continued along the path, Erin now leading the way.

It was now quite dark and the trail had become harder to follow, but the castle lay just ahead. Erin was walking in front of the boys, for some reason feeling quite confident. Not for long though, her next step wasn't so sure footed. She simply disappeared from view, the ground had opened beneath her feet and had swallowed her up whole.

Finn grabbed the strap of Cameron's rucksack, to stop him following.

Erin thudded to the ground beneath them. "Ouch!" she cried out in pain, coming to an abrupt halt.

"Are you alright Erin?" shouted Finn down the hole where she had fallen.

"I think so," came her reply, faintly, "I don't think I've broken anything."

Erin stood up. She had fallen into a huge, underground chamber. Glancing around she realised the chamber was lit by glow-worms—millions and millions of glow-worms.

"Hang on, we're coming," shouted Cameron as he took the length of rope from his rucksack. He secured one end around a large oak tree and dropped the other into the hole.

"You first," he said to Finn. "I've secured it well, there's nothing to worry about."

Finn took the rope and carefully lowered himself into the hole. He could feel Erin grabbing at his legs as he got closer to the bottom.

"Wow! This is amazing!" he exclaimed, as his feet touched firm ground.

The chamber must have been twenty feet deep, a hundred feet wide and at least two hundred feet long. He could barely make out where it ended as everything disappeared into darkness. The glow-worms lit the chamber, but their light faded into the distance, like a beautiful sunset. The air smelled kind of smoky, sweet and sticky, like cider barrels burning.

"Ouch," yelped Finn, as Cameron's feet smacked him around the head.

"Sorry, didn't see you there."

Erin and Finn took hold of Cameron and helped him to the ground. Once down he dusted himself off and looked around, his jaw dropping.

"I can't believe it! This is fantastic!" His eyes scanned the chamber. Reflections danced around them all as the light from the glow-worms bounced off small pieces of coloured glass, set into the solid stone walls. Finn looked to the furthest point in the chamber, where the light faded to darkness.

"There, did you see it? Look there," he pointed into the far distance, "something moved!"

Erin and Cameron looked to where he was pointing.

"I saw nothing!"

"Neither did I, I didn't see anything move."

Finn looked again. Were his eyes deceiving him? Maybe it was just a shadow. Or did something really move?

This time nothing moved. "Maybe not, maybe not." He looked again, but all was still.

"Which way now?" asked Erin, keen to keep moving.

Cameron pointed into the distance, where the light from the glow-worms faded into darkness. "It must be that way, right under the castle. That's our way in."

The three friends sat a while, sipping nettle and damson tea from Cameron's flask.

"I wonder if Willie is in the castle yet?" asked Finn, more to himself than to the others.

"I'm sure he's fine, wherever he is!" Erin placed her arm on Cameron's sleeve. She could see the anguish in his face at the mention of his father.

"Come on, let's get going. We have a lot to do," said Cameron standing up.

The three friends headed off, into the darkness.

"Stay together and we'll be fine." Finn doubted his own words as they set off once more. He was sure he had seen something moving in the shadows.

Chapter 3

THE MOBIUS STRIP

As Willie closed the door to the lodge he muttered his parting words to Cameron, "I'll be back laddie." He desperately wanted to believe them, knowing what lay ahead could claim his life. Willie was not deterred by his thoughts. He was descended from a respected family of hunters and warriors and proudly wore his red, McDougal, tartan over his shoulder. He would not let himself, or Cameron, down. Willie headed through the forest in the direction of Ping castle, focusing on what lay ahead. He remembered a verse his father would say when hunting wild boar. He repeated the verse to himself as he hurried along:

"Fear not where ye are led,
With flowing folds of tartan red,
Yer weapon held within yer heart,
Ye take your role and play yer part.
Yer heart will beat and keep ye stead,
The prize is there within yer head.
On yer return, victorious bound,
The cheering mass the only sound."

The verse lifted Willie's spirit as he repeated it over and over again. By now the sun had all but gone and the dark, evening, sky descended.

Willie reached a fork in the path. '*Strange,*' he thought, '*I can't remember this, which way now? which way?*'

Not wanting to waste any time, he followed the path to the left. He could now see the castle just ahead, in front of him.

A chill ran down his back as he reached the castle walls and laid his hands on the grey stonework. It was as cold as ice and as hard as nails. He followed the wall around, the glow from the moon lighting his path. Finally he reached what looked like an opening. *A way in!* He had come across a completely round hole cut all the way through the wall. The hole was covered by a heavily-constructed iron gate, which was secured with a large, rusting, padlock. Willie tried to move the gate but it would not give an inch. He picked up a large rock which lay close by and began raining blow after blow onto the rusting padlock. Finally, after what seemed like an age, the padlock broke and fell to the ground at his feet. He sighed with relief as he leant against the gate to catch his breath. With his arms still aching from striking the padlock with such force, he pushed with all his might. The gate started to move. Slowly at first, it creaked open, just wide enough to allow him to squeeze through. Behind the gate he found a stone stairway which descended under the wall and into the castle.

Willie suddenly jumped round. Something had spooked him, something from within the forest. He stared into the mass of trees, feeling as if a thousand eyes were looking at him. The sense unnerved him. Not wanting to hang around for too long, he squeezed through the gate and started to descend the stairwell.

****

The walls were wet and the steps slippery as Willie carefully descended, further and further, into the bowels of the castle. The stench was almost unbearable, like a combination of dead rats and mouldy cabbage. The way was lit by burning candles which stood in small pockets carved into the stone walls. As he walked, the candles in front of him ignited themselves, whilst the ones he had passed and were now behind him extinguished themselves. Eventually, after 237 steps (he counted every one) he reached the bottom of the stairwell. He continued along a corridor until he reached a large, circular, room. The walls of the room were lined with mirror. As he stepped inside he could see his reflection a hundred times. Willie waved his arms around, the reflections copied his every move. He started to laugh, his voice echoing and bouncing back off the mirrored walls. He stopped laughing. His voice continued to echo but, instead of fading away to silence, it got louder and louder. Standing in the centre of the room, Willie raised his hands to his head, covering his ears as the laughing penetrated his eardrums. The noise was unbearable, he fell to his knees. Looking up, he saw his reflection—still standing—in the mirror!

"How can this be?" he muttered, amazed at the sight of a hundred images of himself running round and round the room. Willie did not know what was happening. Were his senses playing tricks on him? Was he going mad?

The laughter continued to get louder and louder. The reflections now a blur as they whizzed around him.

"Stop! Stop!" Willie shouted as loud as he could. "By the power within me, I tell ye to stop."

With that the room fell silent; you could have heard a pin drop, it was so quiet.

Willie lifted his head and looked into the mirrored walls. He could see his reflection kneeling in the middle of the room, just as he was. Slowly he got to his feet. Looking ahead he saw the opening through which he had first entered the room. His forehead was furrowed with puzzlement. The way he had entered the room should surely have been behind him, but now it was in front! Was that the way in or, in fact, the way out?

Willie walked over and peered out of the room. Before him was a long corridor lit by burning candles.

"Darn, this must be the way back out!" he whispered to himself, but something did not quite fit right in his mind. Willie did not know if he was coming or going. He remembered the first line of his father's verse, *'Fear not where ye are led,'* and continued to walk along the corridor.

He had been walking for a while when he arrived back at the foot of the staircase.

"Blast," he shouted, as he paused to consider his options. The mirrored room had only one way in and out, so to return to it would be pointless. He decided to climb the staircase back to the castle grounds. From there he would try to find another way in.

He began to climb the stairs. His legs ached and his muscles burnt with the effort of heaving himself up the narrow stairwell. Step after step after step until he finally reached the top. He rested for a while, to catch his breath, before squeezing himself through the iron gate and back out into the castle grounds.

Once more out in the open Willie looked around, his forehead drawn to a point, he frowned in disbelief. He had stepped into a wooded bog and was surrounded by a thick curtain of poisoned vine, ten feet high and several feet thick!

'This is not the castle grounds I know!' he exclaimed to himself, totally confused by what was happening to him.

The bog was dimly lit. Shafts of dark light cast shadows all around. A strange kind of light, it was created by pools of water, which reflected the black moon in the sky.

Willie felt out of control, something must have been playing with his mind, slowly destroying his sanity. He closed his eyes and saw Cameron's smiling face calling to him, "I'll be back laddie." The last words he had spoken to his son. He quickly opened his eyes in an attempt to snap back into reality.

Willie continued to walk through the bog, his legs felt like lead weights as the sodden ground attempted to suck the boots from his feet. He now had no idea where he was going but inside he knew that The Dark Spirit and The Purple Crystal must be getting closer. He continued on, further and deeper into the bog, his body ached and his heart grew heavier.

After a while he came across a large rock and decided to rest. He sat down and took a flask of nettle and damson tea from his sack, along with a piece of homemade herb bread. He drank and ate before drifting into sleep.

****

A bird perched on high in a large oak tree. Its head cocked as its piercing yellow eyes rested on Willie's chest, watching it rise and fall as he slept. Shadows twisted and contorted as the moon cast its darkness over the bog. The Black Hammer was thin and weak, it had not eaten for several days. Its stomach churned at the thought of fresh flesh, Willie's flesh! Silently it fell from its perch, tucking its wings in tightly as it got closer to Willie. The Black Hammer struck, sinking its razor sharp talons into Willie. He awoke immediately, startled by the attack.

"Be gone ye foul evil thing." Willie frantically thrashed his arms around knocking, the bird to the ground. "Ye'll not be taking my soul tonight," he shouted at the bird as it righted itself and flew off into the distance.

With all the commotion Willie barely noticed a Shellac appear from under some bog fern. A Shellac is a small creature, not more than three feet tall. Quite hideous looking, it had overgrown ears and a large nose, which curved onto its chest. It was dressed in a tatty webbing tunic which was full of holes and wore shoes made of cloth, tied with string. The Shellac had lived in the black forest since leaving his family home, many moon phases ago, scavenging for food, eating anything he could find. The Shellac grabbed Willie's sack and made a quick escape into the bog. Willie, catching a glimpse of what was happening, leapt in the direction of the Shellac and landed directly on top of it, pinning it to the ground.

"I'll have that," snarled Willie, grabbing back his sack, and holding tightly on to the Shellac.

"Please don't hurt me, don't know what came over me, meant nothing bad." The Shellac looked frail and tired, he had a pale, varnish-like, complexion and protruding, crooked teeth. His large eyes pleaded with Willie.

Willie lifted his large frame off the Shellac, expecting him to run. The Shellac didn't move, he lay quite still, all the energy drained from his body.

"Hungry, weak, didn't mean to take sack. Don't know what made me do it."

"You could have asked," replied Willie, still reeling from the Black Hammer attack.

Willie took pity on the small; frail; creature and handed over a large piece of herb bread. The Shellac took the bread and started to eat. It was the first time he'd ever experienced generosity in his many years of living in the bog.

"What might I call ye?" asked Willie.

The Shellac looked surprised. No one had ever called him by his name, not since leaving his home in a quest to avenge his parents' deaths. "Lackey," he replied.

"Pleased to meet ye Lackey, I'm Willie, Willie McDougal. I have no quarrel with ye and I'll be gone in the morning when it gets light." Willie passed Lackey his flask of nettle and damson tea. "Drink this, it will make ye feel better."

Lackey took Willie's flask and drank, until his small belly could take no more.

Lackey felt refreshed after eating and drinking, he was clearly undernourished and happy to have some decent food in him. He stared at Willie. He had never seen anybody so large and powerful-looking with such a kind nature.

"Don't get much lighter than this," Lackey's voice trembled as he spoke. "Bog always... in shadow. Sun and moon one of a kind, have been since Dark Spirit came amongst us." Lackey's face contorted with the sheer effort of speaking of The Dark Spirit.

"You know where he is? You know where I can find him?" asked Willie, his ears pricking up at the very mention of The Dark Spirit. Lackey grinned slyly. "Here with us now, sees everything, hears everything. The Black Hammer his eyes, the wind his ears."

Willie's jaw dropped open. "He can see us?"

"Yes. When Black Hammer attacked he saw the fear in your face, but also determination in your eyes. Lackey saw it too!"

Willie's voice boomed with anger. "But you know where he is?"

Lackey's eyes filled with hatred. "Castle is his fortress—for now."

He pointed to the eastern walls, "Somewhere in there."

Willie looked puzzled, "Why do you say 'for now'? Speak little man, speak." Willie grabbed Lackey by the arm.

"Please don't hurt Lackey, Lackey tell you everything."

Willie released his grip.

"Dark Spirit grows in strength every day. Has fed on departed souls for many moon phases. Soon will unleash his power over our world and yours, casting them into darkness forever."

Willie clenched his teeth, "I must stop him, I must."

Lackey's eyes widened, "Impossible, Lackey tried for many moon phases."

"Nothing is impossible, can you get me inside the castle? nothing more, just inside?"

Lackey fell silent. He had lived much of his life in silence, having initially being struck dumb. Emotionally scarred, his speech still impeded by the actions of The Dark Spirit, this could be the chance he had been waiting for. His chance for vengeance! He looked into Willie's eyes, reflecting on the generosity he had shown towards him. "Yes, Lackey help. Lackey show the way."

Willie smiled, passing his flask back to Lackey. "Drink up little friend, you will need all the strength you can find."

Lackey took the flask and drank. "Must head north of castle, then we cross The Mobius Strip!"

"The Mobius what?" asked Willie.

"The Mobius Strip. It is way into castle, a single-sided walkway made from skulls of departed."

Willie felt his throat tighten and his palms began to sweat.

"Spans The Ocean of Evil. Them'll try and drag us in, pull us under. One slip means end—over. Them'll eat us, feed our souls to him!"

Willie stood up abruptly.

"Right little friend let's get going," he said, offering his hand to Lackey and pulling him to his feet.

"This way, Lackey show," said Lackey as they headed off, into the bog.

The undergrowth got thicker and Willie struggled to keep up with his small friend. Lackey's nimble footwork allowed him to race through the bog. "Slow down!" shouted Willie, "I'm busting a gut here!"

Lackey paused a while to give Willie time to catch up. "Must hurry," insisted Lackey. "Mobius Strip only passable for short while. We miss our chance—will have to wait another seven moon phases."

They continued on their way, Willie trying to keep Lackey in his sight at all times.

"Watch out for bog-weed!" shouted Lackey, pointing to clumps of crimson bushes. "Its grip is lethal!"

Willie and Lackey continued to travel swiftly and silently through the bog, getting closer to The Mobius Strip.

"Ahead, look... I see it," said Lackey, pointing to a stretch of water in front of them.

The water looked black, almost like ink. It gave off an odorous smell of decay. A thin grey walkway spanned it, stretching all the way to the castle entrance.

"I see it; The Mobius Strip; I see it ahead." Willie's voice was a mixture of excitement and trepidation as they reached the water's edge.

"Stay hidden," beckoned Lackey to Willie. "Stay under frizzle tree." Lackey pointed to a clump of trees growing on the water's edge. "Him'll see us, we stay out too long. Remember him has eyes everywhere."

Lackey pointed skywards where a Black Hammer flew overhead.

Willie quickly took cover under the trees; their gooey sap stuck to his face and matted his hair.

"Careful not to get sap in mouth, tastes like honey but will give you bellyache for a week!"

The two companions sat under the tree and rested for a while. Willie removed a small bar of chocorice from his pocket, to share with Lackey. It was Willie's favourite, a combination of the finest Swiss chocolate and the richest Scottish liquorice root. A 'must' from the Ping sweetie shop. Full of energy, a weekly treat for Cameron and himself. Thoughts of his son pained him as he wondered when...no, if, they would ever meet again.

The chocorice was unlike anything Lackey had ever tasted before, its sweet flavour lingering in his mouth, he savoured every morsel.

"Must go," Lackey stood up. "Make sure clothes are secure. Tuck loose clothing away, less they have to grab hold of, is better."

Willie heeded Lackey's words, tucking even his boot laces inside his boots.

Lackey took hold of Willie's hand, his small fingers barely long enough to wrap around Willie's thumb. "Listen to me Willie!" his voice now sounding confident, trusting Willie. "I lead, you follow. Must move quickly, stay close to Lackey, have faith in your strength, as I do in my nimbleness."

Lackey's words reassured Willie, although he still wasn't sure what he was about to do.

"Once we step onto The Mobius Strip, can only go forward. Do not bother yourself looking back. It will no longer exist! Listen to Lackey."

Willie clasped his hands around Lackey's, "I fear nothing and will protect you, my little friend." His face was calm, his eyes showed no fear.

Lackey stepped onto The Mobius Strip, he felt the icy cold water of death as he started to walk. Willie followed, his legs turning weak and heavy with trepidation. The vile water started to lap at their feet, stinging and nipping their toes. A penetrating wind started to blow making their progress slow and dangerous; one slip and they would fall. Willie fixed his gaze onto Lackey as the water started to bubble and froth.

From beneath his feet came a strange shrieking noise. Glancing down he saw the skulls of the departed from which The Mobius Strip was made. Crying and moaning with pain, these bones were all that separated them from the evil water below.

Without warning, a hand rose from the icy depths and grabbed at Willie's leg, gripping tightly around his ankle. He remained focused and strong as he continued to move along the strip. Looking ahead Willie could see Lackey, dancing through the mass of arms and hands which grabbed, desperately, at him.

"Keep strong ma wee friend, move yer nimble feet," he said, fearing that one wrong move would surely result in a watery end for Lackey.

Willie's words of encouragement echoed behind Lackey as the mass of hands continued to claw at him. The water was now white with activity and the shrieking voices of the departed had become even louder.

The hands were now blindly grabbing at their feet, Lackey managed to slip his scrawny legs through any hands that took hold of him. Willie used his great strength to pull himself along, inch by inch, his teeth clenched in determination.

The piercing wind blew ever stronger and the companions struggled to remain upright as the Ocean of Evil started to swell.

A Black Hammer swooped low, brushing past Willie and knocking Lackey to his knees.

"Hurry Willie, must hurry," shouted Lackey. "Him watching, listening to us!" Lackey regained his feet and continued along the strip, the end now in sight.

The Black Hammer circled once more, its eyes scanning like radar, feeding new information back to The Dark Spirit. It hovered high above them, focusing on the weaker of the two. The Black Hammer then started to dive, Willie caught sight of it from the corner of his eye and shouted to warn Lackey of the imminent attack.

"Run Lackey. Run!" Willie's words of warning were too late. The Black Hammer struck, sinking its claws deep into Lackey's back. Lackey screamed in agony as the razor-like claws sank to the bone. The Black Hammer picked Lackey clean off his feet and started to fly towards the castle walls.

Willie had now reached the end of The Mobius Strip and leapt the last few feet, onto firm ground. He looked upwards helplessly as Lackey was carried skywards. Quickly he took his sling shot from his sack. He grabbed a stone from the water's edge and placed it firmly into the sling, whirling it around and around his head to gather momentum. Willie concentrated hard on the evil bird as he released the stone. He held his breath as it glided, silently and quickly, through the air, knowing he would not get another chance. The stone struck a deadly blow with clinical accuracy contacting with the Black Hammer's head.

Lackey fell, lifeless, into the Ocean below. Willie, with no thought for his own safety, followed Lackey into the water. He managed to grab his arm and pull him to the water's edge where he lifted him onto firm ground. The spirits of the departed swarmed upon Willie, desperately trying to pull him under the water to claim his soul. He used his size and strength to defend himself as he pulled his mass onto the ground next to Lackey.

The two friends lay a while, Willie catching his breath, filling his lungs with air. Lackey remained motionless.

"That was a close one!" Lackey did not reply. "Lackey, Lackey." Willie shook Lackey in an attempt to rouse him.

Lackey started to murmur faintly. He was still alive.

The wounds on his back were deep and oozed with thick, green, blood. Willie reached into his sack and removed a small cloth bag, tied with string. He opened the bag and removed a small handful of slackweed. Willie often used slackweed, as it was renowned for its healing powers; ideal for cuts and grazes. He squeezed the slackweed, allowing the oil from its leaves to drip onto the open wounds on Lackey's back. He gently rubbed the oil in, then covered the wounds with the leaves before binding them tightly around Lackey's body with his tartan scarf.

"Rest now ma wee friend, nothing will harm ye now." Willie supported Lackey's head as he helped him to sip some nettle and damson tea from his flask.

"Thank you Willie, you saved Lackey's life. I shall be ever—

indebted to you." Lackey closed his eyes; tired and weakened, he slept.

Willie sat by his friend's side, protecting him from the icy wind, covering him with his coat to make him comfortable. He found a moss-covered stone and placed it under his head for a pillow.

He looked back along The Mobius Strip. The Ocean of Evil was now calm, like a lily pond. Not a single ripple in sight to lap the shore. The icy wind blew strongly, but not even that could penetrate the water's marble-like surface.

Willie smiled to himself. He neither knew where he was going, nor how he would get back, but he was pleased to be alive and happy to have finally found a way into the castle.

Chapter 4

LETHAVIAN PING

As Finn, Erin and Cameron, slowly made their way to the far side of the chamber, the light from the glow-worms started to fade and their eyes had to strain to see the way.

"This is no good, soon we will see nothing!" said Cameron, pausing to speak to his friends. "We need a torch." Cameron reached into his rucksack and removed the glass jar of mints. He offered the mints to Erin and Finn before tipping the rest into a handkerchief and stuffing them into his pocket.

"What are you doing Cameron?" asked Erin in puzzlement.

"You'll see!" said Cameron, as he set off, retracing his steps back into the chamber. Once far enough in, and surrounded by thousands of glow-worms, he removed the lid from the jar and stuffed it full of the tiny insects. He cut a length of lace from his boots, made two puncture holes in the top of the lid and threaded the lace through, tying it tightly with a slip knot. He then quickly replaced the lid before any of the glow-worms had chance to escape! He had learnt to tie a slip knot when hunting with his father, great for snaring rabbits. Cameron then returned to where Finn and Erin were standing, holding the glass jar up high by its lace handle. The worms cast a dim—but useful—light across the dark chamber, just enough for them to see their way, but no more!

"Brilliant! Now we have a torch." Finn smiled at the ingenuity of his new friend.

The three continued, the chamber becoming narrower as they went, forcing them to walk in single file.

Cameron now led the way, guided by the light from his glow-worm torch, whilst Finn brought up the rear. The tunnel they were now walking through was cold and damp, icy drops of water dripped down on them as they walked. The air was filled with the stale smell of neglect and it became quite slimy underfoot, causing them to slip and slide along. It wasn't long before the smell became much stronger, reeking of decay and death!

"I'm frightened!" exclaimed Erin, "we don't know where we are, or where we're going."

Cameron stopped and held the glow-worm torch nearer to Erin as a tear ran down her face.

"You're right Erin, we don't know exactly where we are, but we do know we are getting closer. We must get the Purple Crystal before The Dark Spirit turns day into night forever!"

Cameron wiped the tear from Erin's cheek. "Don't worry, if we stick together we'll be fine. I will make sure of that, as will Finn."

Finn nodded in support as Cameron turned to continue along the tunnel.

The glow-worms continued to light their way. Unaware, they were now walking somewhere under the Ocean of Evil, with Willie and Lackey quite close by, somewhere above them.

As they walked along they could hear a droning noise in the distance, it got louder and louder the further they walked. In the far distance they could see something glistening, beams of light dancing around, bouncing from side to side. The noise increased to a thunderous volume as they came to the end of the tunnel and stepped into another chamber. This chamber was a lot smaller than the one housing the glow-worms, and partially filled with water. A narrow lip of a walkway encircled the chamber, twenty feet or more above the water's surface.

The three friends stood in silence, now aware of what was making the noise. A huge cascade of water poured down from somewhere above, crashing into the plunge pool below. The black water boiled with activity as the Ocean of Evil thundered down in front of them. The water, alive with movement, seemed to writhe as if in agony.

Finn stared into the water.

"There's something in there!" he said, pointing at the water as it erupted in a torrent of froth and bubbles.

Cameron and Erin joined Finn staring into the murky depths below.

"Look, something's moving!" shouted Erin, as a black, slimy, head arose from beneath the water's surface.

"What's that?" she asked, as the two boys looked on, dumbstruck.

The head, which was the size of a man, steadily rose, exposing an array of razor-sharp teeth, grimacing at them from atop of a long, thin, amphibious-looking body.

All three stood frozen to the spot, not even daring to breathe since the creature appeared to be smelling the air above it. Finn's footing slipped slightly as the thin walkway on which they were standing suddenly crumbled from under his feet.

"Careful Finn!" shouted Erin, her heart pounding heavily, as both she and Cameron grabbed hold of Finn to stop him falling into the water below.

The creature lifted its head and lunged at where they stood. Foul-smelling drool oozed from the creatures mouth, through its teeth which snapped shut with enormous strength, narrowly missing Cameron.

"Stand still," whispered Finn as the creature's jaws snapped in their direction once more.

"It can't see us, it's reacting to noise," whispered Finn, through clenched teeth.

The creature circled on top of the water, before diving below the surface and out of sight. All three sighed with relief as they edged off the walkway and back into the mouth of the tunnel.

"What was that?" asked Erin, her heart continuing to pound as she spoke.

"It looked like some sort of snake, but I've never seen teeth like that before!" Finn trembled with fear as he spoke.

"Look, over there!" Cameron pointed to the far side of the chamber, his eyes straining as he peered through the cascading water.

"Look, you can see a light coming from over there; it must be the way into the castle." His face became etched with determination at the thought of reaching the castle.

"We must get past this creature, we must get to the other side. The walkway will take us around the edge of the chamber to where the light is coming from." Finn pointed at the narrow walkway which was no more than two feet wide and which in places, was starting to crumble into the water below.

"I'm happy to lead," said Finn, volunteering to guide them round. He was nervous but he knew it was the only way.

Cameron took the mints from his pocket and offered them to Finn and Erin. Cameron sucked hard on the mint, trying to clear the noxious stench from his nostrils.

Finn cautiously stepped out onto the walkway. He pressed his back hard against the damp wall behind him and slowly began to edge his way around. Erin followed just a few steps behind. Cameron put his rucksack on back to front and quickly followed Erin.

"Careful Finn," said Erin, speaking as softly as she could, not wanting to alert the creature.

Finn made his way along, back pressed tightly against the wall. He took great care when he passed small sections of the walkway that had crumbled away. Making sure to alert his companions to the danger.

"Finn, ahead." Cameron nodded ahead, indicating something with his eyes, "that gap is too big for us to pass!"

A large section of the walkway had crumbled, worn away by the constant spray from the Ocean of Evil as it cascaded down.

Finn stood still, forcing Erin and Cameron to stop also.

"We can't get past that, it must be seven or eight feet wide. Even if we jumped, we can't be sure how secure the walkway is at the other side!" Finn spoke as quietly as he could, aware that if the creature heard him, it would attack.

Disheartened, but not completely discouraged, the three friends—now led by Cameron—edged their way back to the mouth of the tunnel. Once again on firm ground they sat and collected themselves since they were all suffering from nervous exhaustion.

"We can't get past that gaping hole. If we jumped, the walkway would probably collapse." Erin lowered her head into her hands as she spoke, frustrated by their predicament.

"It probably would under my weight!" Cameron smiled, trying to make light of the situation.

"We must try the other way—to the left—and hope that there are no gaps in the walkway at that side!" Finn pointed in the other direction, his outstretched finger following the edge of the chamber.

"But what if there *are* gaps, what if we can't get passed. Then what will we do?" Erin looked to the boys for answers.

"Then we go back and try to find another way in." Cameron's voice sounded upset as he spoke, saddened by the thought of having wasted so much time when he knew time was against them.

"We're not giving up now," said Finn, as he prepared to try again.

"Come on, I'll lead." He stepped onto the walkway. Erin followed closely behind, then Cameron, as they slowly started to make their way around.

All three pressed their backs firmly against the wall of the chamber, looking only at their feet and not at the murky water below them. They moved slowly and silently, not wanting to alert the creature, as they stood just feet above its watery home.

Finn carefully felt every inch of the way. Cautiously testing each step as he went, ensuring he did not send any of the crumbling walkway into the water. Glancing ahead, he could see that the walkway was unbroken.

"Careful as you go, it could give way without warning," said Cameron, whispering to his friends.

Finn now had the end of the walkway in sight. The light that they had seen through the cascading water shone brighter. Finn could see that it was candlelight, from what looked like another tunnel exiting the chamber.

Finn's confidence grew as he got closer to the end of the walkway, each step became wider and his caution diminished. A smile erupted across his face, *'We've done it,'* he thought.

The smile, however, was soon replaced by a look of sheer horror. The walkway suddenly gave way beneath him and he began to fall towards what was, almost certainly, a watery grave.

As he fell, he frantically waved his arms about, desperately wanting to grab hold of something; anything!

Erin screamed in horror, but her brother's fingertips managed to locate part of the walkway which was still intact, saving him from falling further—if somewhat abruptly.

"Quiet Erin, we must keep quiet!" But it was too late. As the words left Cameron's mouth, the water erupted. The creature's head, quickly followed by its torso, leapt from the water towards them.

The creature snapped and spat at Finn's legs, missing them by merely inches.

"Erin you must remain silent, it can hear us. That is the only reason it knows where we are, it heard your scream!" said Cameron quietly.

Erin had to struggle, more desperately than the boys could have imagined, just to stop herself from making the slightest whimper.

The creature kept attacking, having now also picked up their scent. It continued to lunge at Finn; snapping its menacing teeth, it managed to rip his trouser leg.

"Quickly grab an arm," instructed Cameron, as he grabbed hold of Finn.

Erin quickly took hold of her brother and between them they strained, with all their might, to heave him back onto the walkway.

The creature lunged towards them once again, now smelling their fear, knowing it was close. Its teeth made contact with part of the walkway just behind where they were standing, crushing it like candy!

Finn swung his legs upwards and with one final effort Cameron and Erin managed to pull him onto firmer ground.

The creature attacked again, but was suddenly distracted by a clapping sound, which echoed around them. It paused for a while, straining to identify where the noise was coming, from before lunging towards the walkway at the other side of the chamber.

Cameron, Finn and Erin, stared at where the creature now focussed its attack. There stood an old man, dressed in what looked like a jewel-encrusted cassock. He had a flowing white beard, but little hair on the top of his head. The old man stood, clapping his hands together, smiling to himself with amusement. The noise of the clapping continued to echo around the chamber, confusing the creature.

"Keep moving, we're nearly there," said Cameron, urging his two friends on, as they stepped off the walkway and into the opening lit by candlelight.

"We've made it," sighed Erin, clearly relieved to be off the walkway and away from the water's edge.

"Ah yes, you have made it, but where now?"

The three friends span around, to see the old man now standing before them. His face was pale and weathered, no doubt from his many experiences, but he had a friendly smile and did not appear to pose a threat to them.

"Who are you?" demanded Finn, with new found authority.

The old man smiled, "why I am the reason you and your two friends are here, there *are* three of you aren't there?"

"Off course there are three of us, can't you see?" Erin's response came quick and sounded a little harsh.

"No my dear I can't. I haven't seen a thing since Lethavian took not only my liberty, but my sight also!"

Erin hanged her head in shame for the way she had spoken to the man who, in fact had saved them from the creature.

"You say you are the reason we are here. Then who, are you?" asked Cameron inquisitively.

"I, my dear boy, am Theodore Ping. Ruler, or should I say, ex-ruler, of this land!"

"Theodore Ping, but you're supposed to be dead! You died years ago for meddling with the afterlife—or so they say," said Cameron, now looking somewhat bemused.

"I most certainly did not die, but I did come very close. That night remains etched in my mind as if it were only yesterday." Theodore looked pained as he spoke, his memories clearly disturbed him.

"You must be hungry, you have travelled far. Come, follow me. Do not be afraid," he said. As he turned, he clapped his hands together. The dark, marble, wall in front of them split into two, exposing an opening.

"Quickly, this way," said Theodore as he walked through and disappeared into the darkness beyond.

The three friends looked at each other. Erin, not wanting to offend Theodore again, took the initiative and followed him, the two boys close behind.

Theodore led them down a narrow corridor which brought them to a large wooden door. He stopped and removed a silver key which hung from a chain he wore around his waist, underneath his cassock. He placed the key into the lock and turned it, twice to the right and then three times to the left. He then removed the key and placed it back underneath his cassock.

"Home at last!" he exclaimed in a loud and forthright voice. With that the door swung open and he stepped inside.

"Come along, come along," Theodore beckoned to the three friends, "step inside, hurry, hurry! you don't know who might be watching!"

Erin, Finn and Cameron walked through the doorway and into Theodore's home. The door slammed shut, locking itself behind them.

They had stepped into Theodore's home, which appeared to be carved from solid marble. A roaring fire danced and crackled along one wall, spitting sparks of light into the air contentedly. There was a large sofa in the room and several, imposing-looking, armchairs. A carved, wooden, bookshelf took pride of place, domineering the entire room. It was full of books, hundreds and hundreds of books; spreading wall to wall and floor to ceiling. Theodore clicked his fingers, instantly the room was lit by many candles, the light from which was increased as it reflected off the smooth marble walls. The floor was bare, apart from a solitary rug, resembling a wild animal, which was spread in front of the fire. The animal rug had staring eyes which followed you, no matter where you went. In one corner of the room was a small, metal framed bed. Next to it there stood a bedside table, covered with piles of gold coins. Most of the visible walls were covered with pictures, the majority being of Ping castle and its surrounding countryside. The largest, and most prominent, picture was one of two men, stood side by side, dressed in tartan robes.

"Who are they in your picture?" asked Finn, pointing at the two men, forgetting that Theodore could not see, as his curiosity got the better of him.

"The one on the left, my young friend, is me in happier times," said Theodore as he busied himself preparing tea and cake for his new guests. "And the chap on the right, well he... he... is the other reason why you are here."

"What!" exclaimed Cameron, not quite understanding Theodore's meaning.

"The chap on the right is my younger brother—Lethavian, Lethavian Ping." Theodore's smile disappeared as he spoke.

"Your brother, does he live here with you?" asked Erin innocently.

Theodore's smile returned and he started to chuckle.

"Well my child yes, I suppose he does live here with me—or, should I say, his presence certainly does."

"What? I don't quite understand. Is your brother dead?" asked Cameron, desperately trying to work out Theodore's meanings.

"If only he were!" replied Theodore, who continued to chuckle.

"Perhaps you would understand me more if I were to call my brother by his other name. You see, you may know him as The Dark Spirit!" Theodore's smile disappeared once more, the words obviously left a bitter taste in his mouth.

"*He* is your brother? *The Dark Spirit* is your brother?" said Cameron, gasping with shock.

"Alas yes, Lethavian Ping, The Dark Spirit, is indeed my younger brother."

"Come; come and sit by my fire," said Theodore as he carried a tray of hot, steaming, tea and slices of his favourite ginger and honey cake, placing them on a table in front of the sofa. He sat down and poured himself a cup of tea.

"How do you do that?" asked Erin.

"Do what my child?" replied Theodore, a little bemused.

"You walk around freely, you make trays of tea and cake, you haven't bumped into anything and yet you say you can't see!" said Erin, sitting down with a slice of cake.

Theodore smiled. "I have lived here for more years than I care to remember. I could tell you where everything is in this room, it is all up here," he said pointing to his head, "everything is up here, all mapped out."

"Then why do you stay here if you can make your way around? Why do you allow your liberty to be controlled by Lethavian?" Finn sounded angry as he spoke.

Theodore looked saddened. "Because, my child, I have never managed to venture further than where I met you, I have my limits!"

Theodore passed around the ginger and honey cake, as the three friends helped themselves to the tea.

"So why did Lethavian, The Dark Spirit, imprison you here?" asked Cameron, his mouth bursting with tea and cake.

"A good question my boy—and one I will try to answer. Now; where shall I begin?" Theodore stroked his long white beard as he pondered his response.

"Lethavian and I grew up here, in Ping Castle. We had, I must say, a very happy childhood. My mother died sadly, giving birth to Lethavian. My memories of her are now as grey as my beard.

Lethavian is just two years younger than me and so we played together and enjoyed similar things. That, unfortunately, came to an end around the time of my sixteenth birthday, with the death of my father." Theodore sipped at his tea, trying to hide his pain behind his cup as his memories came flooding back.

"An accident, so they said. He fell from the castle walls, broke his neck!"

The three friends listened with great interest as Theodore continued.

"From that day on things were very different within the walls of Ping Castle. I tried to continue with as much normality as I could; Lethavian, on the other hand, withdrew himself completely. He spent most of his time locked away in his room, reading books about witchcraft and the afterlife. He hardly spoke, only appearing for food every now and then. On my eighteenth birthday the deeds for the castle passed to me, as I was the eldest surviving child. I owned everything, including the Purple Crystal of Ping."

"The Purple Crystal! you have it?" said Finn excitedly.

"I did, but sadly not any more. You see the crystal held many secrets and many powers, the likes of which I just was not interested in. I threw myself into my own studies, one day hoping to become a member of the clergy. Lethavian became jealous, I had everything he wanted; the castle, the crystal, even a career. I, of course, was happy to share everything with him, but he was not happy. The more I focused on the light and the good, the more he focused on the dark and the evil. I would often sit outside his room, trying to strike up a conversation with him, but he would never respond to me. He chose to spend hour after hour in isolation, often talking to himself. He would throw things around in his room; day and night no longer existed for him, he slept when tired and paced around when not. He became pale and thin, his eyes turned yellow with evil, his hair, long and black—and his teeth rotted."

Erin slipped her hand into Finn's, trying not to let her fear show.

"It was Lethavian's eighteenth birthday—I had just turned twenty—when he came looking for me. How that night remains with me."

Theodore's eyes welled with emotion.

"He found me, sitting quietly in the library, reading. I could see the anger in his face as he approached, his words still as clear as the moment they left his lips."

'I am eighteen brother, time to take what is rightfully mine.'

"He lunged at me, grabbing the Purple Crystal and ripping it from around my neck. I had worn it for as long as I can remember, not once taking it off." Theodore grabbed at his chest to where the crystal had once hung.

"How could he steal from his brother," said Erin clearly disgusted.

"He took more than the crystal that night my dear." Theodore stroked his beard again as he spoke.

"He raised his hand to me, muttering words which I found unfamiliar. A blinding light shot from his hand, piercing my eyes, taking my sight forever. The only sound I could hear, was Lethavian's menacing laugh." Theodore's head dropped into his hands and he clasped his ears. "And this is where he sent me, to this marble tomb, somewhere beneath the castle. Lethavian took everything, my home, my eyes—and even my life. Thankfully he left me with my soul." Theodore began to chuckle, "So here I am, with just a few rats and, of course, Lethavian's serpent for company. Remarkable how you got past it, many have tried but you, my young friends, are the first to succeed—my very first guests."

"So what happened to Lethavian?" asked Cameron, not wanting the story to finish.

"Lethavian has spent many years feeding on the souls of the departed, fuelling his power, waiting to release it. Over our world. The Purple Crystal protecting him from anyone, or anything, that tries to stop him becoming the most powerful source of evil to have ever existed."

"So when I Cameron take the crystal from him, then what?" asked Cameron, fearing nothing.

"An almost impossible task, especially for one so young." Theodore spoke with admiration for his new found adventurous, friends.

"But if we manage to, then what?" Cameron persisted, determined to get Theodore's answer.

"If the crystal is taken from Lethavian, then.. then," Theodore hesitated as he spoke, "then he will loose power and strength. But you must understand, even without the crystal, Lethavian is evil itself!"

Silence fell over the room. Finn swallowed hard, trying to untangle the knot in his throat. Erin looked pale, and Cameron was lost for words.

"Enough now; eat, drink and rest yourselves, you have a lot to consider." Theodore offered more tea and ginger and honey cake.

"The time for Lethavian to unleash his power is here, isn't it Theodore?" Cameron knew that it would not be long before Lethavian would start to spread his evil and destruction across Scotland—and beyond.

"Yes my child, the time is close."

"Then we continue. I would rather die, than succumb to The Dark Spirit and live my life in a world of evil." Cameron enjoyed his life with his father in the forest and would not let anyone take it away from him.

Theodore smiled, "I knew you would come, I knew you would. I have waited a long time for this moment. I knew you would come."

Finn and Erin looked at Cameron, "we started this together, we finish it together." The words left their mouths at exactly the same time, their minds working as one.

Cameron smiled. "That twin thing is spooky, feel the same, think the same; now that is *real* power."

"I knew, I knew," said Theodore, as he busily collected a selection of books from his bookshelf. "Come now, we must plan, plan our route." He placed the books on a large table next to the doorway of the room and clapped his hands. A candle ignited, on the wall just above the table, giving off just enough light for the three friends to see.

"Come now, come see my books. I have maps of the castle. We must plan our route."

Theodore smiled excitedly as Finn, Erin and Cameron stared at the heavily-bound books which were covered in a hundred years worth of dust.

"*Our* route, what do you mean *our* route, Theodore?" asked Erin.

"Of course *our* route, you don't think after waiting all this time that I would let you go alone?" Theodore's face broke into a huge smile. He had waited for—even dreamt of—this day coming, he would not let it pass him by easily.

"Come my three young friends, listen to my books."

"Listen?" exclaimed Finn, becoming confused with what Theodore was saying.

Theodore opened the first book. Cameron's jaw dropped in surprise at what he heard next.

"Ping Castle. Built fourth of September, sixteen hundred and eighty five, by Sir Marcus Ping, first Laird of this land. Architect, nobleman and follower of white magic."

"The book is speaking I can't believe it, a talking book!" Erin laughed nervously as she spoke, doubting her own ears.

"Fourth of September!" said Finn listening on in disbelief.

Theodore stood chuckling to himself. "Believe it my friends, this is the largest collection of talking books anywhere. Go on turn the page."

Erin carefully passed her hand over the book, took hold of the page corner and turned it over.

"Ping Castle master plans; including first floor level, entrance hall, the Stag and Armour room, the Tartan Drawing room, Minstrel Gallery and Billiard Chamber." The book spoke, uninterrupted, until it fell silent.

"Turn another; go on, turn the page," Cameron urged Erin to continue, mesmerised by the book.

Erin took hold of the next page and, again, gently turned it over.

"Ping Castle master plans; including the Firing Gallery, Ocean Room, and the Marble Crypt." The book then fell silent once more.

"That's it, the Marble Crypt, this must be the Marble Crypt." Theodore spoke quickly, excitement getting the better of him.

"We must leave this place, pass through the Firing Gallery and across the Ocean Room. That will take us further into the castle—and closer to Lethavian." Theodore now spoke with a serious edge to his voice. "My books will be our guide; and you, my friends, will be my eyes."

"We will?" asked Finn.

"Yes Finn, we will," replied Cameron, eager to get moving once more.

Theodore was now busily preparing refreshments for the journey. He wrapped slices of ginger and honey cake, wild boar sandwiches, and fig pie, as Cameron refilled his flask. Everything was placed into Cameron's rucksack—taking care, of course, not to damage the phials of pixie pogrom. Erin and Finn looked on, both aware of what each other was thinking, and nodding to give each other reassurance.

"We must go quickly my friends. This way." Theodore made his way to the opposite side of the room from where they had entered. Cameron, Erin and Finn followed. In front of them stood a solid marble wall.

"Where are you leading us?" asked Finn, still unsure about what they were about to do.

Theodore did not reply, instead he clapped his hands three times. The wall in front of them started to move, a slight tremor at first, but one which got louder as the slabs of marble separated, creating a hole, right through the wall.

"This way, guide me through," said Theodore, stretching out his arm.

Erin did not hesitate, she took Theodore's hand and walked through, Cameron and Finn close behind.

Chapter 5

THE FIRING GALLERY

The three friends, and Theodore, now found themselves walking through a passageway, somewhere beneath the castle. Candles lit their way, slowly burning, seated in small niches carved into the solid stone walls. It wasn't long before the passageway started to slope downwards. The slope soon became so steep that steps started to appear every few feet, until gradually the passage had gone and they found themselves descending a stone stairwell. The stairwell twisted and turned the deeper it went. The air became dry, it became quite a task just to breathe.

"I can't go any further," Erin stopped and sat down on one of the steps. "It's getting too hot in here." A bead of perspiration rolled down her forehead, stinging the graze left by the Black Hammer.

"Rest a while child, but then we must continue. The firing gallery cannot be much further." Theodore placed his hand on Erin's shoulder.

She knew he was right but she still needed to rest for a moment.

Cameron removed a flask of lemon water from his rucksack. "Drink this, it will stop you from dehydrating," he handed the flask to Erin who drank before passing the flask to the others.

Finn now led the way, with the others eagerly following. After just a few more minutes of descent the steps came to an end and the passageway opened up into an area at least a hundred feet square. The temperature in the room was so hot, it was almost unbearable. The heat seemed to come from a giant furnace, which roared furiously, bursting with flames, and which sat smack in the middle of the room. The furnace was completely surrounded by a moat of—what appeared to be—mud. The mud bubbled and boiled, plumes of noxious gas escaping from it.

"So this is the firing gallery! I rather expected guns and a place for target practice," Finn grinned, amused by his own comment. Meanwhile, Erin and Cameron stared into the flames.

"No my friend, the firing gallery houses only one thing," Theodore paused to compose himself before continuing. "the flames of evil, the very gateway to hell itself!"

Finn, Cameron and Erin, stood in silence as Theodore spoke. "If we do not destroy Lethavian and take the Purple Crystal, then all his power and hatred will be unleashed from this very place."

Another bead of perspiration ran down Erin's cheek. It mixed with a tear as it dripped from her face. She was scared, angry and confused. She feared for her own life, as well as for the lives of her new friends and her family. "We must find him, we must." Her voice trembled as she spoke.

"Can you see a way out, past the furnace? There must be a way through, somewhere!" Theodore asked his three new friends.

They strained to see past the furnace; there was plenty of light in the room, coming from the flames as they danced and jumped, twenty feet or more, into the air. The heat, however, was relentless; it dried every drop of moisture from their eyes as they searched for a way ahead.

"I see a stairwell leading upwards, and a..." Finn blinked, in an effort to get moisture into his parched eyes, "an archway—possibly a doorway—it's hard to tell; my eyes feel like they're on fire."

"Then that's where we must head, to the stairwell." Theodore gave the instruction and the four set off, towards the furnace.

As they got closer to the moat of mud it started to bubble furiously, giving off sulphur and smelling of rotten eggs. Suddenly a torrent of mud erupted skywards. A single figure emerged from it and stood, motionless, on the surface of the mud. The first torrent of mud was quickly followed by another; and then another... and another... until six figures stood before them. The figures were seven or eight feet tall, with no discernible visible faces. They appeared to be made of the very mud from which they came, and upon which they now stood in total silence. The figures resembled the human form, each holding a lethal-looking sword in one hand. The swords were made from a curious-looking black metal which reflected prisms of dark light as the flames from the furnace reflected off their razor-sharp blades.

"Stand perfectly still," said Cameron, as he quickly explained to Theodore what was happening.

"Ah, I expected something to appear. You don't think the gateway to hell would be left unguarded, do you?" Theodore smiled, happy to be having a taste of danger injected into his, hitherto, solitary and uneventful existence. "Mudthogs! They are Mudthogs. Lethavian's foot soldiers and first line of defence. They feel nothing, see nothing and hear nothing, yet they are aware of everything!"

The three friends swallowed hard as Theodore's words had sent a shiver through each of their bodies.

"They obey no one except Lethavian. He created them and he controls their minds; they do as he alone commands."

"How do you know all this?" asked Cameron in puzzlement.

Theodore smiled, "my books of course. My speaking books, they tell me everything."

The Mudthogs started to advance, their feet gliding over the surface of the mud until they reached firmer ground. They then continued to move towards the frightened group, who remained frozen to the spot. Ironically, in a room so hot, they felt as if they were melting.

"How do we destroy them?" asked Finn.

"We, we can't. Only Lethavian, their master, can do that."

Cameron quickly removed his catapult from his rucksack, along with several stones. He placed one of the stones into the sling, pulled back the elastic and aimed at one of the Mudthogs. He concentrated hard, he didn't want to miss and waste even one stone. The sweat from his brow ran down his face, stinging his eyes as it went. He released the stone which flew swiftly toward the advancing Mudthog, striking its forehead with pinpoint accuracy. The Mudthog's head exploded, particles of mud splattered in every direction.

"Good shot," shouted Erin, impressed by Cameron's aim.

The, now headless, Mudthog stood motionless whilst its fluid body remoulded itself to form another head.

Cameron's jaw dropped open, "impossible, I don't believe it, how can that be."

The Mudthogs continued to advance.

Cameron again placed a stone into his catapult and drew back the elastic. This time he focused his shot on the hand of one of the Mudthogs—a hand which held a lethal-looking black sword high above its head. He closed one eye, folds of skin puckered on his brow as he frowned with concentration. The sweat continued to run off him as he released the stone. It shot swiftly through the air, again striking with pinpoint accuracy. The Mudthog's hand exploded.

Globules of mud splashed into its body and its sword crashed to the floor. The sword sliced into the ground, like a hot knife sinking into a pot of butter.

"Quickly! Grab the sword," shouted Cameron.

Without even a word of an answer, Finn dived at the Mudthog's feet and grabbed at the cold, black metal, handle which lay before him. The Mudthog's hand had now reformed; it slipped around Finn's neck, its fingers pushing into his throat. Finn felt the life being squeezed out of his body—just as he had in the forest when The Dark Spirit had tried to claim his soul. He could feel the cold metal handle of the sword, now firmly in his right hand. Finn, desperate to live, swung the sword towards the Mudthog. The blade made a whooshing sound as it sliced through the air, into the Mudthog's torso, severing it clean in two. The Mudthog released its grip from around Finn's throat as its two severed halves seemed to dry out instantly, crumbling into two piles of dust at Finn's side.

The other five Mudthogs continued to advance. Finn lay, dazed, on the floor, next to the remains of his defeated adversary.

"Finn there's another," screamed Erin to her brother, trying to snap his conscious mind back to reality.

The words hit his brain like a bolt of lightning and he swung his sword in the direction of the advancing Mudthog. The cold black metal sliced, effortlessly, through its legs. The action of the desiccation came quickly. Every last drop of moisture evaporated from its body at once, turning stone-like before crumbling to the floor. The sword it had been holding fell, point first, sinking deep into the ground where it struck.

Cameron hurried to help Finn to his feet, whilst claiming the discarded sword as his own.

"Take Theodore over there," said Cameron, wiping the sweat from his brow and pointing to where they had first entered the firing gallery.

"Be careful," replied Erin, nodding in acknowledgement of Cameron's order. She led Theodore by the hand, away from the advancing Mudthogs, and to safety.

Cameron and Finn now stood side by side as the four remaining Mudthogs drew closer.

"What now?" asked Finn, "any suggestions?"

Cameron wiped the stinging sweat from his eyes. "I wish my father was here, he would know what to do."

"I wish he was here.... but even if he were, the Mudthogs only seem to respond to the sword."

"You're right, we fight them with our swords; our heads, and our hearts." Cameron felt the blood of his ancestors' surging through his veins as the Mudthogs drew even closer. They smelled of the same vile odour given off from the gases which escaped from the moat of mud.

One of the Mudthogs swung its sword in Finn's direction, Cameron jumped to save him, swinging his sword and deflecting the blow. The black metal sparked like flint as the blades clashed, the force from the Mudthogs blow almost knocking Cameron's sword from his grip.

"Its legs Finn, aim for its legs."

Finn swung his sword, its sharp metal blade slicing legs from body. The Mudthog dropped its sword as its body reduced to dust and fell to the ground in a shower of tiny particles.

Cameron and Finn retreated a little distance. The Mudthogs moved only slowly across the ground, which allowed the two boys time to catch their breath and assess the situation. The heat in the gallery seemed to be increasing as they were soaked with sweat from their efforts.

"Only three remaining, we must fight together, pick them off one at a time," said Finn, straining to get the words out, the heat scorching his throat as he spoke.

Cameron placed his hand on Finn's shoulder as a mark of their solidarity. Their trust was mutual—as was their fear.

Erin watched closely, afraid for their lives, but willing them on. She constantly gave a running commentary to Theodore, who imagined the scene in his head, aided by the sounds of the battle taking place. Erin felt a sharp pain in her stomach. Finn felt the same discomfort, as his intestines twisted with fear.

The Mudthogs were now upon them, the flames of evil reflected in the shaft of black metal as one swung its sword at Cameron.

He managed to block the blow, but the force of doing so sent a pain shooting up his arm, like a bad cramp.

Finn stabbed at the apparition, sinking his sword deep into its stomach. The Mudthog froze, before crumbling to the ground at their feet.

Cameron and Finn could not believe their success; four Mudthogs down... only two to go.

Lethavian had clearly underestimated the determination of two, so young, battling against his evil quest and destroying his foot soldiers with their very own weapons.

"Finn! Cameron! Help!" Erin's cry banished any thoughts of fatigue. They turned to see one of the Mudthogs approaching Erin and Theodore.

Erin cowered behind Theodore as the advancing Mudthog; got closer. Theodore lifted his hand and started to utter words which neither Erin, nor the boys, recognised. The Mudthog hesitated then swung its sword at Theodore.

"Hold tightly to my waist child," he instructed Erin, before continuing to utter at the Mudthog.

The blow, with all its force, made contact with them.....or did it? The blade glanced from them, leaving them unmarked and uninjured in any way. Again the Mudthog swung its sword at them; and again the blade glanced away before its razor-sharp edge could slice into their bodies.

Cameron and Finn reached the Mudthog as it continued to rain blow after blow upon Theodore and Erin.

"Now!" Shouted Cameron, as they both sank their blades into the Mudthogs torso. Its sword crashed to the ground as its body crumbled to dust at Theodore's feet.

"Here, take this," said Finn, as he retrieved the sword and handed it to Erin, "Think of it as protection." He smiled at his sister as she took the sword from his grip.

The boys swung around when a grinding noise from behind them caught their attention. The last remaining Mudthog was approaching them. A sword in each hand, the Mudthog scraped the blades together menacingly. It lunged towards Cameron and Finn, swinging a sword at each of them simultaneously.

They lifted their swords, barely managing to block the blows and almost losing their grip, as the Mudthog continued to attack in a frenzied rage.

The attacking Mudthog was relentless. Both arms working independently, as it rained blow after blow upon its prey.

Finn grunted with the effort of defending himself, his head pounded as he exerted every muscle in his body. Cameron also had to use every ounce of effort he could muster, as the attack was quickly draining the energy from his body and mind. The blade from the sword which was attacking Cameron ripped through his trousers and sliced into his flesh with ease.

"Argh! he got me," Cameron cried out as his legs buckled beneath him, sending him crashing to the ground. His sword fell from his grip and spun across the ground away from him. He now lay at the feet of the Mudthog, exhausted and unarmed.

The Mudthog lifted one of its swords above its head, preparing to strike a deadly blow, while still fighting Finn with its other arm.

It drove the sharp, metal blade, towards the ground; Cameron closed his eyes. He knew his adventure was over and so braced himself, waiting for the sword to enter his body. Thoughts of his father rushed through his mind; he saw his entire life in the blink of an eye. Silence fell as his body was engulfed in a cloud of dust.

He paused for a moment, before flickering both eyes open to get his first glimpse of hell. Looking up, he saw Erin. She stood above him, still holding the sword which, moments earlier, she had sunk deep into the Mudthogs chest, saving his life.

Finn dropped his sword and fell to his knees, "Cameron, are you alright?" he asked, as he glanced at the gaping wound on his friend's leg.

Cameron felt the pain in his leg, but it did not bother him. His gaze remained fixed on Erin, she had saved his life. He should be dead.... maybe he was; maybe this was not real at all. He reached down and touched the wound on his leg; the red, sticky, blood on his fingers was real enough.

"Erin, Erin you saved me." He spoke softly, still dazed by the experience.

Erin dropped her sword as she turned to Cameron.

"We did it," the smile on her face brimming with joy, "we did it." She dropped to her knees and flung her arms around Cameron and Finn.

"You have done well my friends, exceptionally well," said Theodore, standing at their side. "You have defeated Lethavian's foot soldiers, you have weakened him, weakened his defences. He will be watching us."

Cameron cried out in agony, the pain in his leg increasing as the shock of what had happened began to wear off.

Theodore placed his hand under his cassock and removed a small bottle of liquid.

"Try and keep still Cameron, this may sting a little. Erin, place my hand on his leg," instructed Theodore. "Now carefully allowed two drops of the liquid to spill into the open wound," he continued, passing Erin the small bottle.

Erin, did as she was asked, being extra careful not to spill, even a single drop.

"Argh! what is that?" asked Cameron, grimacing as the liquid stung his flesh.

"Liktus lotion, a little something I created myself. Watch your leg." The three friends watched as the wound on Cameron's leg started to heal itself, his flesh knitting together before their very eyes.

"Wow! That stuff is amazing." Cameron ran his hand across his, now unblemished, leg. Not even a sign of the smallest scratch remained. Erin and Finn looked on, mesmerised by the action of the

Liktus lotion.

"That stuff is magic in a bottle," said Erin, as she helped Cameron to his feet.

Theodore smiled proudly, "magic in a bottle... yes it is, magic in a bottle; and only I know the ingredients needed to make it. One of my better inventions I think."

All four now headed towards the archway.

"Come my friends, lead the way. We must leave this place." Theodore stroked his beard as he spoke. They had been victorious this time, but he instinctively knew many more encounters would lie ahead.

As they got closer to the archway, the heat in the firing gallery decreased. The stairwell next to the archway acted like a chimney; sucking fresh, cooler air, downwards from somewhere above them. It felt good to smell fresher air once more, it flushed the remaining noxious odours from their nostrils.

"We must rest a while; eat, drink and ready ourselves for our onward journey." Theodore could feel the exhaustion in his friends growing with every breath they took. "We will rest here and cool ourselves in the breeze."

The four weary souls sat and feasted on the wild boar sandwiches and the ginger and honey cake. They relived the battle with the Mudthogs, talking excitedly about what might lay ahead. Finally they all drifted into sleep. All, except that is, Theodore, who kept an ear alert at all times.

The roar of the furnace hung in the air, it was the only thing that could be heard in the gallery. Theodore suddenly sat bolt upright, something had caught his attention, something in the stairwell. He tilted his head to give his right ear as much exposure to the sound as possible. The sound became louder, almost echoing as it steadily became clearer. Theodore could now hear footsteps, quite clearly approaching them, from the stairwell.

"Wake my friends, wake." Theodore shook all three to alert them to the sound.

"What is it?" Finn sat up, startled by Theodore's voice.

"Shhh! Listen, I can hear footsteps approaching. Listen! In the stairwell..."

Finn and Cameron grabbed the swords they had claimed from the Mudthogs and positioned themselves either side of the stairs, out of sight of whoever was coming. Erin took Theodore's hand. They stood in silence, backs firmly pressed against the wall.

"Mudthogs, thought we'd seen the last of them. Lethavian must have sent reinforcements. You know what to do."

Finn nodded in acknowledgement of Cameron's words.

Both boys stood silently as the footsteps got louder and louder.

"Listen! There are two of them. I can definitely hear two sets of footsteps." Theodore's hearing was extremely sensitive having grown keener, due to his lack of sight.

Cameron firmed up his grip on his sword, pleased that Theodore could only detect two Mudthogs—and not an army of them.

Finn was aware of his heart thumping in his chest as his nerves were once again tested, his courage pushed to the limit.

The footsteps got even louder as they got closer to the bottom of the stairs. Cameron and Finn stared at each other, both holding their swords aloft.

"Now," shouted Finn.

Both boys swung their swords into the stairwell opening.

"What the ...?" Cameron smashed his blade into Finn's sword just before it made contact with Willie, who now stood startled at the bottom of the stairs, Lackey at his side.

"Father!" Cameron's face beamed as he flung his arms around Willie.

"What are ye doing here laddie? I left ye in the lodge, safe at home!" Willie tried to sound angry but could not, he was so pleased to see his son again, alive and well.

"We came after you, to help. We wanted to get the Purple Crystal with you and help destroy Lethavian." Cameron couldn't stop the words racing out of his mouth, being so relieved to see his father.

"Destroy whom?" asked Willie, looking somewhat puzzled.

"Lethavian, Lethavian Ping, my brother. You may know him better as The Dark Spirit."

"Your brother, ye say, and *who* might *ye* be?" asked Willie.

"I, my friend am Theodore Ping, Laird of these lands."

Willie began to laugh. "Theodore Ping, then ye must be dead for he died years ago!"

"No Willie, he did not die. He was imprisoned by The Dark Spirit, blinded by him too." Erin said, believing Theodore. She had no reason to doubt a man who had saved her from the hands of the Mudthogs.

"Well, if ye are in fact Theodore Ping, then it is my honour to meet ye."

Theodore smiled. "And if *you* are Cameron's father, brave Cameron, then it is indeed an honour to meet you too."

Theodore stretched out his hand to Willie, who gladly accepted the gesture.

"And the Shellac..? Theodore sniffed the air as he spoke.

"Lackey; his name is Lackey; and yes he is my companion."

Lackey stood behind Willie, peering around his giant of a friend.

"I thought so, they have a distinct smell, the Shellacs. I can usually smell them a mile away!"

"Come and sit over here with us father, we have wild boar sandwiches and lemon water." Cameron led his father, and Lackey, to the entrance of the archway, where they all sat and ate.

"So how did ye get here ahead of us?" asked Willie.

"We left the lodge not long after you and headed towards the castle. Then we fell into a cavern, just outside the castle walls, full of glow-worms it was. Then we walked along a passage, at the end of which we encountered the serpent. Then we met Theodore, who took us..."

Willie interrupted before Cameron had time to finish his sentence. "Slow down laddie, ye're getting me all confused. A serpent ye say?"

"Aye! It was a hundred feet long, with razor-sharp teeth."

Willie could see the excitement in Cameron's face as he spoke.

"A hundred feet ye say? It must have been a fearful sight."

The conversation was interrupted by the sound of Lackey, snoring, as he drifted off to sleep. The wound on his back still bound with Willie's tartan scarf, but healing well thanks to the slack weed.

"Now you father; how did you get here?" asked Cameron, eager to hear of his father's journey.

"Well I entered the castle through a mirrored room. It was a strange room, didn't know if I was coming or going as the mirrors spun around me. After that I walked through a swamp, that's where I met Lackey. Lackey very kindly showed me across the Mobius Strip."

"The Mobius what?" asked Erin, blankly.

"The Mobius Strip! A narrow walkway spanning the Ocean of Evil! A bit tricky that was, anyway that's when Lackey was attacked by a Black Hammer, nearly claimed his soul it did. From there we entered the castle down the stairwell; six hundred and sixty six steps exactly, I counted every one! And here we are." Willie grinned, happy to be back in the company of Cameron and his friends.

"So we now know the way forward must be through the archway, as the stairwell would lead us back to the Mobius Strip." Theodore stroked his beard as he spoke. "Hence the cooling breeze from above. We must move soon, Lethavian will not rest while we are here, especially now that we have destroyed some of his Mudthogs."

"Mud what?" asked Willie inquisitively.

"Mudthogs, Lethavian's foot soldiers, seven or eight feet tall, made entirely from mud! They can regenerate their own body parts, even heads!"

Cameron quickly interrupted, before Willie had time to reply.

"Yes father, Finn's right. Lethavian's first line of defence—and we've killed six of them between us already." He smiled at Finn and Erin, proud of their achievement.

"Then we must go, before he sends any more Mudthogs after us." Willie stood up, giving Lackey a shake to wake him.

Lackey stood to his feet, close to Willie.

"We must pass through the Ocean Room, that should lead us closer to Lethavian if my books are accurate. It must be somewhere through the archway," said Theodore as he too stood up.

"Ocean Room? Don't like the sound of that—crossing the Ocean of Evil was bad enough." Willie tried not to show his concern to the others, so as not to alarm them.

"This way then, stay together; keep your eyes open for Mudthogs." Cameron took the lead and set off through the archway, a strange—looking archway, made of (what looked like) bone.

After several yards the archway swung sharply to the left. When they turned the corner, they were confronted by a solid wall.

"It's a dead end, there's no way through." Cameron's voice was edged with disappointment.

"Can you get us through this wall Theodore?" asked Erin, taking his hand to position him directly in front of it.

"I don't know my friends, but I will try."

Theodore placed his hand on the cold, damp wall and began to utter more strange words. After which he clapped his hands three times. Nothing happened. He tried once more, but again nothing happened.

"It is no good, I am not able to do anything, it must be protected by Lethavian. We will have to return to the Firing Gallery and look for an alternative route."

Sad and frustrated they turned back, to head towards the firing gallery.

"No, wait a minute. The swords, they cut through stone like scissors through paper," said Erin, as she handed her sword to Willie.

"Well I suppose I can give it a go." Willie held the sword tightly with both hands, he lunged with the blade point first, at the wall. As the blade made contact, it effortlessly sank through the solid stone wall. Willie carefully cut a small doorway into the wall, before removing the sword and handing it back to Erin.

"Well done lassie, yer not as daft as ye look." Willie smiled at Erin before resting his shoulder against the newly cut doorway and pushing with all his might.

The doorway slowly started to move. Cameron gave a hand and together they pushed the doorway back until they had made an opening, large enough to squeeze through.

"Follow me!" Willie stuck his head back through the hole.

"It's a bit miserable-looking through here, but it's better than heading back."

He disappeared again through the doorway, closely followed by Lackey and the others.

Chapter 6

THE OCEAN OF EVIL

Erin, Finn and Cameron now followed Willie as he led them through the doorway he had cut into the solid stone wall. Lackey held Theodore's hand as he guided him along.

Theodore was well known to the Shellacs, who trusted him. They would occasionally bring him wild boar, or rabbits, from their many hunting trips, leaving the animals at the entrance to the serpent's layer. Occasionally Theodore would feast on the spoils of the hunting trip, if the serpent didn't beat him to them! Payment would always be made in gold coin; this amused Theodore, as he was not aware of any reason why the Shellacs would need money.

Cameron, Erin and Finn chatted excitedly, oblivious to where they were now heading. They had encountered and overcome more than they had ever imagined possible, just a few days ago; their heads were now brim full of Mudthogs, Black Hammers and, of course, Lethavian Ping.

"Can you see anything?" asked Theodore.

"Not a lot," replied Willie, "its a bit dingy down here."

They followed a single pathway which disappeared into darkness in all directions around them. In the distance they could hear a faint wailing sound, which served to make the whole situation even more eerie.

The hairs on the back of Willie's neck stood on end. "Don't feel right, not sure what it is, but I don't feel right." Willie stared into the darkness, but could see nothing.

As they continued along their way, the wailing became much

clearer. The noise sounded as though it was not made by only one person—or creature, instead it seemed to be the result of many voices crying out together and it sounded increasingly human. It became quite painful to listen to. Lackey covered his ears with his hands. "Don't like, noise hurts Lackey."

The light seemed to increase slightly, it started to flicker and reflect above them, occasionally catching an eye as it bounced around. The wailing sound was now quite loud; its painful tone had disappeared and it now sounded quite calming, even pleasing to the ear.

Willie began to yawn. "I feel tired out, could do with a good kip."

Cameron and Erin also began to yawn. "Me too," said Erin, straining to keep her eyes open.

"We cannot stop, we must keep going. It is Lethavian, he is playing with us. The wailing is acting like a hypnotic, he wants you to sleep so he can claim your soul." Theodore shouted his words, so as to be heard over the wailing.

"He's right, focus yer minds," said Willie, shaking his head as if to rid the sound from his ears. A beam of light from above caught his eye. He concentrated hard, trying to make out what it was. It flickered again... and then again.

"It's water, the ceiling is liquid, look it's moving," Willie pointed above. The entire ceiling was fluid, seemingly suspended by nothing—but obviously held in place by something.

"The Ocean Room! We are in the Ocean Room! That is what the book said, 'from the Firing Gallery, through the Ocean Room.' At least we now know that we are heading in the right direction." Theodore smiled, whatever lay ahead for them, he knew that he was getting closer to Lethavian.

Erin glanced around as she stood, motionless, beneath the Ocean of Evil. She sensed a thousand eyes staring at her, the same feeling she'd had many times before.

"What's the matter lassie? Ye look like yer've seen a ghost!" Asked Willie.

"We're being watched, I feel like we're all being watched."

Willie glanced around. "I don't see anything," he said, placing one of his huge hands on Erin's shoulder in reassurance.

As they continued further into the Ocean Room, the more seductive the wailing sound became; even Lackey removed his hands from his ear's as he enjoyed the wailings calming effect.

For a while Willie forgot where he was. Enchanted by the wailing, he slipped in and out of a trance-like state of mind. He occasionally shook his head to rid the sound from his mind, snapping back into reality when he did. Only too soon, however, the sound would permeate back into his brain, controlling his thoughts, guiding his actions.

"Father, wake up," shouted Cameron.

Willie now stumbled as he walked, only just managing to remain on his feet.

"Father, wake up," shouted Cameron again, but his words did not register with Willie, who suddenly fell to his knees and then flat onto the ground.

Willie lay quite still, his eyes fixed above, mesmerised by the water. He wore a broad grin on his face as he listened to the wailing which to him, now sounded like the most beautiful bird chorus ever, singing softly in his ear.

"Father wake up! Come on, wake up." Cameron tried, unsuccessfully, to rouse his father. Willie now lay, oblivious to anything around him—except for the sweet music gently flowing through his mind.

"Theodore, can you not do something?" asked Cameron, scared for his father.

"I cannot my child, Willie is under Lethavian's control, he has let him into his mind." Theodore looked angry—angry that his own brother could be so evil.

"We must continue. If we remain here for much longer, Willie will not be the only one of us to succumb to Lethavian." Theodore was determined not to let that happen.

Lackey sat at Willie's side. "Not leaving friend, Willie saved Lackey, not leaving him." Lackey bowed his head when speaking, not wanting to make eye contact with the others.

"Grab an arm, we will drag him along, it will help us to focus. Come on, let's get going." Cameron reached down and took hold of his father's left hand and forearm. Erin guided Theodore to Willie's arm at the same side as Cameron, while she and Finn took hold of the other arm.

"Ready.... Pull!" Finn gave the order and all four started to drag Willie along the ground.

Lackey darted from one side to the other, trying to help where he could, but his feeble size and effort made little difference. Progress was slow and, although it did help to block the wailing sound from their minds, the sheer effort soon overpowered them, forcing them to stop after only a few minutes.

"That's it I've got to stop, I can't go any further, I'm exhausted." Erin collapsed to the ground as she spoke.

"We will rest a while before we try again—we can't give up that easily." Finn placed a reassuring hand on Erin's shoulder. He smiled at her warmly, his eyes becoming quite glazed as the wailing gently passed through his ears and into his mind.

'THWACK!' Erin slapped Finn around his face.

"Ow! What was that for?" he asked, somewhat dazed.

"That, my little brother, is to wake you up! I don't want to have to drag you as well as Willie."

Finn rubbed his cheek, which by now was quite red and sore.

"I know what to do," shouted Cameron as he removed the handkerchief full of mints from his pocket. He opened the handkerchief and offered them around. "Take two each and stick them in your ears."

Cameron shoved a mint into each ear. "There, I can hardly hear a thing," he bellowed at the others.

The others followed Cameron's example, Lackey needing two mints for each of his large ears. Rather disgustingly, (to Erin at least) Lackey chose to lick each mint before inserting them in his ears.

The wailing sound did not seem to have that much effect on Theodore but he took a mint anyway—although he popped his in his mouth. "Mmm, peppermint, my favourite."

Willie lay quite still as he continued to be mesmerised by the wailing. His eyes were fixed on the liquid ceiling, the surface of which moved constantly, rippling to and fro. The sound of the wailing became obsessive the more Willie concentrated on it, its seductive powers drew him in—like a bee being drawn to the sweetest of nectars. Willie was now captured by the wailing. His head, his heart and his soul, were no longer his to command. He felt his body becoming lighter as he was slowly drawn closer to the liquid ceiling.

"Willie," shouted Finn as he leapt to his feet, grabbing a leg, just as Willie's entire body left the floor and began to float upwards, towards the Ocean of Evil.

Erin and Cameron quickly followed suit, jumping to their feet and grabbing a limb each; both of them startled to see such a monster of a body floating, completely unaided.

"Theodore! Lackey! Help us!" Shouted Cameron, desperate not to let his father be taken from him.

Lackey quickly stood to his feet. He unravelled the tartan scarf from his body, the one used by Willie to bind his tiny body after the Black Hammer attack. Lackey held tightly to one end of the scarf, throwing the other end over Willie's body. He grabbed the free end as it fell back down to him and tied both ends together in a knot. He then sat in the loop he had made, determined that his tiny Shellac frame *would* make a difference.

Theodore stood beside them. Raising both arms, once more he started to utter in a different tongue. His voice becoming throaty as he repeated his words over and over again, "Wairua tohunga levisia, wairua tohunga levisia."

Willie's upward movement halted, now he simply hovered in mid-air—several feet above the others.

Cameron, Erin and Finn maintained their grips, whilst Lackey hanged in his tartan loop below his friend's body.

"Keep going Theodore, it's working," pleaded Cameron.

Theodore continued with his chant as Willie's body slowly started to descend back to the ground.

The liquid ceiling then began to move, in a frenzy, above them. The water bubbled and frothed as if angry with them. Hundreds of arms pushed their way through the surface of the water, waving and grabbing at Willie.

"What is that?" asked Erin, the colour draining from her face.

"Soulless bodies; claimed by Lethavian, entombed in Ocean forever. Him not stop until him has claimed all of us."

Lackey now realised that they were under the same stretch of water both Willie and he had crossed just a day earlier.

Willie's body again started moving upwards, towards the water. Theodore continued to chant his words, a picture of Willie clear in his mind—but it was no good.

"I can't do it." He felt weak from the effort, the energy from every muscle sapping away from him. "He is too strong for me." Theodore had strained his body and mind battling with the very evil of his own brother, Lethavian.

Theodore managed to continue for a few more moments before collapsing backwards to the ground; his spell, as well as his spirit, broken.

"Father, father," shouted Cameron, his words wasted as he tried in vain to hold on to Willie, who now drew closer to the water above him.

"It's no good, I can't keep my grip." Erin's fingers felt as if they were being pulled from their sockets, her toes barely touched the floor. One by one, all three... let Willie slip through their grip as they fell, against their wills, back to the ground.

Lackey remained attached to Willie by the tartan scarf.

"Lackey, jump! We can't save him," shouted Finn.

The words only just managed to get past the sticky mints still lodged in his ears. "Willie is Lackey's friend, Willie saved Lackey.

Lackey not leave friend." He gripped tightly to the scarf as he continued to be drawn upwards with Willie, getting closer and closer to the water.

Cameron, Finn and Erin, could do little but watch as the frenzy of arms beckoned them closer, grabbing at them and pulling them in. The frenzy continued, erupting like an inverted volcano blowing its top for the first time. Willie and Lackey were pulled into the ocean, the water engulfed them and they disappeared from sight.

Silence fell, the wailing stopped, and the liquid ceiling became quite still again.

Cameron sat with his head in his hands, quietly sobbing. Erin and Finn sat, stunned; not quite believing what had happened. Theodore also sat in silence, drained by the spell he had used in the vain attempt to rescue Willie.

"My father, he has gone." Cameron's words cut like a knife, making everyone feel his pain as though it were their own.

"I'm sorry Cameron, there was nothing more I could do, nothing more that any of us could have done." Erin placed her arms around him, wanting to ease his pain, wanting to make everything alright.

Cameron stood up and wiped his eyes, "Maybe he'll be OK. Lackey will help him, just as he helped Lackey."

"I'm sure he will be fine. Willie will not be taken easily, he is a brave man, just like his son." Theodore smiled as he spoke. He knew how it felt to loose a father so dearly loved—and to the same hand that appeared to have just claimed the lives of Willie and Lackey.

Finn removed the flask of lemon water from Cameron's rucksack and drank before offering it to the others, all eager to quench their thirsts.

"Where now Theodore?" asked Erin.

Theodore stroked his beard, "we must continue through the Ocean Room. To where... I have no idea. We must refer to my speaking book."

Erin pulled the book from the rucksack and opened it at the page which had told them of the Ocean Room.

'Ping Castle, master plans, including the Marble Hall, Firing Gallery and the Ocean Room.'

"Turn the page Erin," said Theodore, urging her to continue.

Erin carefully took hold of one corner and turned the single sided page over.

'Upon leaving the Black Forest you will enter the inner evildom of Lethavian Ping, The Dark Spirit. From there, no further records exist.' The book then fell silent.

"From leaving the Black Forest? but we haven't even reached it yet."

Finn continued to stare at the book, waiting for more information—but it held its silence.

"There's a page missing. Look, it's been ripped out!" said Finn, pointing to the page numbers, which read one hundred and twelve, followed by one hundred and fourteen. "See, page one hundred and thirteen is missing."

"Theodore, the page has been removed!" exclaimed Erin.

Theodore looked puzzled. "I have no answers my friends as to its whereabouts, nor indeed, do I know *why* the page is missing."

"It doesn't matter anyway. We just have to continue the way we are already going until we find Lethavian; and when we do I will destroy him, destroy him for the sake of my father." Cameron's sadness had now been replaced by anger and sheer hatred for The Dark Spirit. He would let nothing stand in his way, to prevent him rescuing Willie.

The four friends continued on their way under the Ocean of Evil. Erin took Theodore's hand and guided him along, whilst Finn tried to comfort Cameron as his mind twisted and turned with rage.

The light in the Ocean Room started to increase the further they walked. The liquid ceiling gently moved above them, reflecting magical spectrums of light which danced all around them, the colours lighting their way like fireworks exploding in a dark winter sky. The air became fresher and carried the scent of damp heather starting to warm in the sun. It helped to lift Cameron's spirit as the smell reminded him of home.

Finn spotted something on the ground just ahead of them; he cautiously approached, before bending down to pick it up. Holding it up, he could see that it was a tartan cloth.

Cameron quickly grabbed it from him, "Its my father's tartan scarf," he shouted, as his eyes began to well once more.

"But Lackey secured it around them both, maybe they escaped, maybe they're not dead." Cameron's mind started working overtime, trying to work out why the scarf was here and beginning to think that everything might be alright after all.

"Willie! Willie! Lackey! can you hear me?" Erin shouted, looking around in all directions.

"Father! Father! We're here It's me, Cameron"

All four listened for a response, but non came.

Cameron wrung the remaining water from Willie's scarf and slung it proudly over his shoulder. "He's alive, I know he is; Lackey too. I know my father and he would not leave us."

The find lifted the hearts and spirits of them all.

Chapter 7

◇◇◇◇◇◇◇◇◇◇◇◇◇◇◇◇◇◇◇◇◇◇◇◇◇◇◇◇◇◇◇◇◇◇◇◇◇

SHADOW DEMONS

Willie continued to rise towards the Ocean of Evil, the frenzy of arms still grabbing at him. As the icy cold water touched his face it sent a bolt of reality flooding through him, instantly waking him from his trance-like state.

"What the..." were the only words he managed to speak before he was pulled into the stale, black, water.

Lackey, still attached by the tartan scarf, followed him in.

Lackey now gripped firmly to his friend's leg. Both strained to see through the water, but its dark, murky, depth blocked most of their visibility. The scarf became tighter, but still managed to work its way up Willie's body until it lodged under his arms.

Suddenly they started to move, something had attached itself to the scarf, and was now pulling them along. They moved calmly but with speed; cutting through the water like a torpedo, fixed onto and closing in on its target. Lackey struggled to keep his grip on Willie's leg, since the pressure of the water bore down on him like a ton weight.

Hundreds of streaks of white light started to pass all around them, like a mass of shooting stars. Still they continued to race through the water with increasing speed.

Willie's lungs were now at the point of bursting out of his chest; he desperately needed to breathe, but could not.

Lackey remained attached to his large friend, (Shellacs are able to hold their breath for several minutes underwater, with the longest ever time recorded being twenty seven minutes and thirteen seconds) the thought of breathing had not even entered his head.

Willie felt down the side of his leg until he reached his boot; he carefully managed to slip his fingers far enough inside it to allow him to remove his trusted hunting knife. With the handle firmly in his grip, he thrust forward. The sharp blade easily cut through the tartan scarf, releasing him from its hold around his body and sending them both spiralling backwards, away from whatever had been pulling them along.

As their momentum slowed, they found themselves suspended in the murky water and surrounded by hundreds of human-looking faces, with flowing ghost-like bodies, everyone of which was smiling at them. The faces were completely white, apart from their eyes, which looked tired; dark and sunken.

Willie simply sat in the water, suspended, not daring to move. The pain in his lungs had gone. In fact, the very urge—or indeed need—to take a breath had gone. He wasn't sure what was happening, but the figures started to move their arms, beckoning them to follow. Willie tried to make sense of what was going on around him, but his mind was in such a jumble. Were these the same figures that had tried to pull them off the Mobius Strip, the same ones that had pulled them into the water from the Ocean Room? the streaks of white light that had passed them moments earlier?

"Come! Come! Help us.... free our souls."

Willie shook his head, not knowing if the voice now speaking to him was in, or outside of, his mind. His senses were completely befuddled by hearing so true and clear a voice...underwater.

"Come! Come! Follow us, free our souls from The Dark Spirit."

The white figures surrounded both Willie and Lackey, some pulling them along, whilst others beckoned to them. Suddenly they started to move upwards, getting closer and closer to the upper surface of the water. Willie felt a hand pushing something into his pocket.

"Take our spirits, free our souls, release us from our icy tomb. Help us, please help us."

With that Willie and Lackey erupted through the surface of the water as hundreds of hands forced them upwards, pushing them onto dry land by the water's edge.

Lackey turned, just in time to see the mass of hands sink back into the black water and disappear from sight.

Willie lay spluttering, gasping to get oxygen back into his lungs. Lackey sat in silence, staring at the water's surface.

"Lackey, are you ok?" asked Willie, regaining his breath.

"Yes friend, Lackey fine."

"Did you hear the voice?"

"Yes, Lackey heard," he answered, continuing to stare at the water's surface.

"They want us save them from Dark Spirit," he continued.

"But who are they?" asked Willie.

"Empty shells, trapped in watery grave, souls claimed by Dark Spirit. Lackey help them."

Willie lay back upon the grassy bank at the water's edge. The air smelt fresh, but damp. The light was dusky and an eerie silence hung around them, not even a bird could be heard.

"Do you know where we are Lackey?" asked Willie, his bearings lost.

"Lackey know this place. Lackey been here before. Now in Black Forest, close castle's heart."

"The Black Forest, you say." Willie murmured, trying again to work out recent events and gathering his thoughts. "Where are the others?"

"Lackey not sure, somewhere beneath us."

"Why were we in the water?"

"The wailing noise, captured you, pulled you in, Lackey followed, stay with friend."

"The wailing; yes I remember, it was beautiful," said Willie. Remembering having something pushed into his pocket, he quickly placed his hand in, only to pull out a large round stone, white and silky smooth.

"Lackey look, they gave me this when I was in the water. 'Take our spirits and save our souls,' that's what they said, 'save our souls.' What did they mean? We must find Lethavian and destroy him, maybe then their souls will be free." Willie's mind began to race, '*how can we do that when we don't even know where Lethavian is.*'

"How Lackey, how can we do this?" he asked, not knowing where to find the answer.

"Lackey knows where to find answer."

"Where?" asked Willie, excited by Lackey's response.

"Narabius. Narabius the wise, him will know."

"Who?" asked Willie.

"Narabius, very wise Shellac elder. Him tell Lackey what to do.

"Where can we find this...Narabius?" asked Willie, keen to continue on their way.

"Lackey know where to find him, Lackey show you." Lackey gave a wry smile as he spoke. He felt useful and needed, something he had never felt before, it was strange but pleasing.

"Narabius lives in moss caves at Sirius. Lackey take you there, through Black Forest, on the boundary."

"The boundary? The boundary to what?" Willie was confused, he did not enjoy the feeling of being lost and, although he trusted Lackey, he felt out of control.

"The boundary separates your world from my world. Dark Spirit, destroy boundary if him not parted from Purple Crystal. Only way to stop him."

"How far to Sirius?" asked Willie, eager to get going.

"Not far, one moon phase," replied Lackey, pointing at the sky.

"Moon phase? What is that?" asked Willie, totally bewildered.

"Time it takes for moon to circle sky." Lackey made a circular motion with his bony finger outstretched.

"I think in your world you call it one day."

Willie smiled, pleased by the knowledge that Sirius was not too far away. In fact, he thought one day to Lackey would only be about half a day to him. He felt confident that he could cover the ground a lot faster than his small friend.

"Come on Lackey, let's get going. I'll carry you on my shoulders, should speed things up a bit."

Lackey looked nervous at Willie's request. "Must be careful, Black Forest has many dangers and Lethavian has many eyes." He cowered as he spoke; he had witnessed first-hand the dangers it held and knew that many more of its secrets were yet to be discovered.

Willie was not deterred by Lackey's concerns; he offered his hand to him and helped him onto his back.

"Right ma wee friend, which way?"

Lackey pointed ahead and to the right, "that way to Sirius, through the heather bog."

"Hold on tight wee man," said Willie, as he set off in the direction Lackey had pointed.

He walked briskly, wanting to save as much time as possible. Lackey clung to Willie's back, his arms wrapped around his neck, his little hands clasped tightly together as they bounced along.

The forest remained in semi-darkness. The only light was given off by the black moon which cast a strange glow, and, an array of shadows and shapes, which danced around them. Willie caught a glimpse of something out of the corner of his eye. He stopped momentarily to catch his breath, staring at where the movement had caught his eye.

'Shadows trying to deceive me,' he thought, laughing, unconcerned by what he maybe hadn't seen.

"Must keep moving; can't stand still; danger all around." Lackey's voice was filled with uncertainty as he urged Willie to continue.

"Don't worry ma wee friend, it's only a few shadows." But still the hairs on the back of Willie's neck stood on end as he spoke. His heart started to pound, like someone banging a drum in his chest. He span around and looked into the forest, unnerved. He felt as though a thousand eyes were watching them.

"Keep moving," urged Lackey again, "we must not stop."

The feeling soon disappeared thankfully and they continued in the direction of Sirius.

Lackey sniffed the air, his nose had picked up the scent of the heather bog, not far ahead of them.

"Heather bog, Lackey smells it, not far," he pointed the way as he spoke for Willie to follow.

A Black Hammer sat high on the branch of a large oak tree; its yellow eyes scanned the forest, like radar seeking its target. The bird cocked its head as its eyes landed on Willie and Lackey below. The bird sat quite still, its gaze fixed, following them through the forest below, feeding the image back to its master... Lethavian.

Willie and Lackey continued towards the heather bog, which lay just ahead of them, unaware that they were being watched from above.

The Black Hammer silently fell from its perch, wings tucked tightly by its side. Gathering speed, it approached its prey. The strike came so quickly, and so gracefully, executed that it took both... Willie and Lackey... by total surprise. The Black Hammer sank it claws, painfully, into Willie's shoulder.

"A-A-R-G-H. Get away you evil sparrow," screamed Willie, thrashing his arms at the bird as it took flight once more, back into the camouflaged safety of the forest.

In the confusion of the attack, Lackey was thrown from Willie's back. He landed heavily in a pile of bog-weed, which instantly took a hold around his delicate frame, tying his arms and legs tightly, pinning him to the undergrowth.

"Lackey, are you ok?" asked Willie, concerned for his small friend.

"Lackey fine, bog-weed broke fall. Lackey trapped in bog-weed."

Willie removed his hunting knife from down the side of his boot and walked over to Lackey. Severing the bog-weed he released his friend. As Willie bent down to Lackey, something caught his eye; he quickly span around to see hundreds of shadows, dancing in and out of the trees.

"Willie run, shadow demons."

Lackey's cry came all too late. Willie fell backwards having received a blow to his stomach. Winded but unhurt, he got back to his feet. He was now completely surrounded by shadows; menacing and evil-looking shadows. Willie could not believe what he was seeing,

'Shadows made by what?' he thought as he received another blow to his body, delivered by the hand of one of the shadows. The force of the blow sent Willie reeling backwards, almost falling over Lackey as he went.

"How do I fight them?" he asked Lackey.

"Shadow demons cannot be fought; they exist only in our minds." Lackey's words confused Willie even more than he already was.

"But.... but you see them too! They aren't just in *my* mind."

"I see Willie, with fear in his eyes, nothing more."

"Then why did you tell me to run, as if I were in danger?"

"Willie in danger, from himself. Most, have shadow demons in their minds, ones that come out at night. Hide in nooks and crannies, they do. Deceiving, tormenting you."

Willie shook his head.

"Na, that can't be true. If they exist only in my mind, then I wouldn't have felt the blows, and I certainly wouldn't have been knocked off me feet."

"Willie, no longer in his world; you in my world, Lethavian's world—he knows your weaknesses."

Willie looked around as the shadows swarmed about him, like bees around a honey-pot. He tried to stand back up but the shadow demons attacked again; they pounced on him and pinned him to the ground. The mass of demons on his chest forced the air out of his lungs; he felt hands, slipping around his throat, teasing and tormenting him, just as Lackey had said.

"Willie must relax, think of good things. Listen to Lackey; Lackey want to help."

Willie now lay pinned to the ground. He tried to relax; he closed his eyes to rid the demons from his mind, but could not. The hands around his throat began to tighten as he became weaker, allowing the demons unlimited access to his mind. Willie had always wanted his parting thoughts to be of happy times, his heart bursting with pride for his son. What had become of his life? Where had he gone wrong? No happy thoughts, no proud memories, just shadow demons stealing his life away from him.

"Willie, Lackey still here, clear your mind, release the demons."

Lackey's words echoed in and out of his head as his grip on reality started to slip. Willie now lay quite still, seemingly accepting his fate. He felt an overpowering burning sensation in the pocket against his leg. The sensation increased, burning into his leg—and searing into his mind. The sensation momentarily forced the demons to one side, allowing Willie to muster just enough energy to place his hand into his pocket. He felt the smooth white stone, given to him in the Ocean of Evil by the empty spirits. The stone was hot, and it sent a calming feeling throughout his body. He slowly removed his hand from his pocket, the stone firmly gripped within it.

Willie held the stone above him, his arm outstretched. It shone brighter than any star he had ever seen, spreading daylight all around. The stone lit up the entire forest, banishing all trace of the shadow demons and freeing his mind.

Lackey closed his eyes, he had never seen such a bright light, they just did not exist in his world of darkness.

"Lackey still trapped by bog-weed," he said, looking up at Willie, shielding his eyes from the bright stone with his arm.

Willie, exhausted by his experience, pulled himself to; and knelt by Lackey's side. Using his hunting knife he severed the rope-like weed from Lackey's fragile limbs.

"Lackey thank Willie, once more, Lackey very grateful."

Willie stood back to his feet, also helping Lackey to his. He still held the smooth white stone firmly in his hand, it had altered his perception and freed him from his own demons.

Willie was now even more determined to rid the earth of Lethavian and repay the debt, not only to his own kind, but also to the empty spirits that had saved him from himself by giving him the stone.

Lackey now led the way as they continued the journey to Sirius; the stone lit their way and kept any shadows out of sight.

"Heather bog; Lackey sees heather bog just ahead."

They both stepped out of the forest and into a great expanse of bog land. The bog was extremely wet and muddy underfoot, but its sweet scent was pleasing to the nose.

"This way, Lackey show you. This is why Lackey told you to run from the demons in the forest."

Willie looked puzzled. "What d'ye mean?"

"Shadows don't exist in open, only in shady places."

Willie smiled at Lackey, offering his hand to help him onto his back.

"I will never doubt ye again ma wee friend. If Narabius is half as wise as you; then we shall soon find The Dark Spirit."

They continued through the heather bog, the moss caves almost in sight. After only a short distance, Lackey's eyes lit up; a fluttering sensation filled his stomach. He was home.

"Lackey see the moss caves, look." He stretched out his arm, his finger pointing to a large opening in a huge rock now just in front of them.

"We've made it, this must be Sirius," said Willie, a large smile spreading across his blotchy red face.

"Yes this is Sirius, but we still have to find Narabius," replied Lackey, still sitting on Willie's back as they entered the mouth of the cave.

It was dark and damp, Willie began to laugh to himself, "so this is why you call it the moss caves." He ran his hand down the wall around the cave's entrance, it was lined with dark green moss, easily four inches thick. It felt smooth and luxurious, like an expensive carpet. It was soaked with moisture, which ran down Willie's arm.

"Will ye look at that, me sleeves soaking now." He removed his hand from the moss and wrung the water from his shirt.

"Try the water, taste is good," said Lackey as he pushed his face into the carpet of moss and began to suck the water from it. Willie watched his small friend for a moment before following Lackey's lead, burying his face deep into the moss and drinking the crystal clear water held within it. Willie quenched his thirst before removing his face from the moss.

"Tastes nearly as good as burn water."

Lackey looked at Willie and began to laugh in a high-pitched chuckle.

"What is it?" demanded Willie, "what ye laughing for."

Lackey continued to chuckle, Willie grinned, he had never seen Lackey laughing before, it pleased him.

"Your beard," chuckled Lackey "Its not red anymore...beard green now!"

Willie grabbed at his chin and removed a handful of moss which had become stuck to his beard.

"Laugh at me will ye, wee man?" Willie threw the moss at Lackey, which landed and sat on his head like a covering of green hair. Willie started to laugh, loudly.

For a short while they both forgot the seriousness of their quest and relaxed, enjoying each other's company. They sat for a while on the floor of the cave, sharing a rather soggy wild boar sandwich, given to them in the Firing Gallery by Cameron.

"Right Lackey, let's get going, find this Narabius bloke," said Willie as he stood to his feet.

Lackey joined him and they set off, deeper into the moss cave.

"Do you know where ye're leading us?" Willie asked Lackey as the cave divided into a series of tunnels and walkways.

"Lackey knows the way. Lackey brought up in the moss caves."

Willie had complete faith in his small friend and happily followed.

After several more minutes of tunnels (and weaving in and out of walkways and openings) they arrived in front of—what looked to Willie like—a solid gold door. The door was about ten feet high and almost as wide, fixed with the largest hinges Willie had ever seen. It was guarded by two Shellac warriors, all of three feet tall, wearing full body armour and each holding a jewel-encrusted axe.

"Willie wait here," said Lackey as he approached the Shellac warriors.

Willie stood, watching silently, as Lackey engaged the warriors in conversation. He spoke with them for several minutes, glancing back and pointing towards Willie several times, before removing four gold coins from his pocket and giving the Shellac warriors two each.

"Willie, come quick. We must enter now," shouted Lackey.

Willie rushed to his side.

The Shellac warriors heaved open the solid gold-looking door, allowing both Willie and Lackey to step through.

Chapter 8

NARABIUS THE WISE

As Willie stepped through the gold-looking door, the sight that greeted him left him gob-smacked; in total awe. As the door slammed shut behind them, he found himself standing in the thriving heart of the moss caves, with thousands upon thousands of Shellacs going about their daily business. The Shellacs weaved in and out of doorways, tunnels and walkways, like blood pumping through veins, all moving in one direction with smooth and effortless momentum.

"Lackey welcomes you to Shellac kingdom. Here we find Narabius."

Willie stood silently, unable to speak, his eyes absorbing as much detail as possible as he tried to take everything in. The Shellac kingdom was a huge chasm, carved deep into the rock. Its walls stretched a hundred feet high and tapered into the distance for as far as Willie's eyes would allow him to see. Cut into the walls were thousands of openings, each one home to a shellac family. The openings were only accessible by a series of walkways which weaved up and down, back and forth and side to side. In the centre of the chasm, at ground level, was a busy and thriving marketplace selling an array of goods; food, clothes, bags, purses, swords, even handmade moss boots, were all on display and ready for sale.

"Well I never," said Willie, finally finding his voice, "you live here?"

Lackey nodded, "Lackey lived here when younger, Lackey not been back for many moon phases. Willie, follow Lackey," he said as he hurried off into the busy marketplace, further into the Shellac kingdom.

Many of the Shellacs stopped what they were doing to stare at Willie as he passed by—towering above them.

"Hello Lackey, who's your friend?" Asked one of the Shellacs, waving to Lackey as they passed.

"Hello Fibius, long time no see. This is Lackey's friend, Willie."

"Willie eh? Strange-looking thing isn't he," said Fibius, laughing to himself.

Willie snarled at Fibius, startling him and causing him to fall backwards off the stool on which he was sitting.

"Willie, come this way," said Lackey as he continued to lead them through the market place.

Finally they reached a walkway which took them upwards, towards the Shellac dwelling caves. Lackey stopped when they reached the third level of the caves, "this way, just along here," he said, as he began to lead Willie around the walkway, passing directly in front of the Shellac homes.

"Hello Lackey."

"Glad you're back safely Lackey."

"Never thought I'd see you again Lackey! This is a nice surprise," were just some of the things said to Lackey and Willie as they passed the entrances to the Shellac dwelling caves. After just a few more moments, Lackey stopped at the entrance to one cave in particular.

"Lackey home now; welcome, Willie, to my home. Please come in."

Lackey and Willie stepped into the cave, straight into the kitchen area. The kitchen was softly lit by the flames of a stove, burning in one corner. Gently bubbling away, a large kettle simmered on its top.

Willie had to stoop to enter the cave; and, once inside, he had to hunch his shoulders to stop his head hitting the stone ceiling above him.

A rocking chair creaked away in another corner of the room as it slowly moved backwards and forwards. Willie could just about make out the shape of a small figure sitting in the chair, gently rocking. The poor light did not allow him to see the person in any great detail, but it appeared that, whoever it was, they were even smaller than Lackey.

"Lackey, is that you son? Is that my Lackey?" The voice sounded frail and tired.

"Yes Coralada, Lackey home," he said as he rushed to the chair and flung his arms around his aunt.

Lackey's parents had been taken when he was very young. They said that Black Hammers stole them from within the forest, claiming their souls for The Dark Spirit. Lackey had been thrown into a bush of bell-heather by his mother as the Black Hammers had attacked, a desperate act, but one which had probably saved his life. He was found several days later by Shellac tribesmen, returning from a hunt. They brought him safely back to the Shellac kingdom, where his aunt Coralada took him under her wing. The only memory Lackey had of his parents was of the greenstone pendant that they would hang over his crib at night to keep the evil spirits away—the very same pendant he had worn proudly around his neck ever since the Shellac hunters had returned him to his aunt.

"Lackey, it has been so long," said Coralada as she tightened her grip on him.

"Yes aunt, but Lackey back, for now!" Lackey was clearly pleased to see his aunt after such a long time, to be reunited with the person he held in the same esteem as his own mother.

"Aunt this is Lackey's friend, Willie," he said, nodding in Willie's direction.

"Any friend of Lackey's is very welcome here," she said, extending her hand to Willie.

"Pleased to meet ye Coralada," replied Willie as he took the frail, thin, hand into his own.

"Please sit by the stove, I have moss-weevil soup cooking, you must have some."

"Sounds different," said Willie, "but I won't say no, I'm starving."

Willie and Lackey both sat down, each one onto a small wooden stool. Coralada rose from her chair, scurried over to the stove and dished up two steaming-hot bowls of moss-weevil soup. She handed the soup to the hungry pair, along with a chunk of homemade stonebread, before returning to her rocking chair.

"Eat up, don't let it cool too much," Coralada smiled as she spoke, happy to have Lackey home at last.

"Aunt, Lackey sorry, but can't stay long. We have come to speak with Narabius."

Coralada's eyes widened with surprise at the very mention of Narabius's name.

"We need help aunt, time has come. Dark Spirit is almost ready, must destroy him." Lackey's eyes filled with tears as he spoke. Avenging his parents death now had much wider-reaching consequences than he had ever imagined. Not only would his own world decline, but so too would the world of his friend Willie, if

Lethavian was not stopped.

Coralada's memories returned to the day that Lackey had been brought to her by the Shellac hunters. The death of her sister, Lackey's mother, had been eased by Lackey's innocence. From that day on Coralada became a full-time mum; raising Lackey to know right from wrong, supporting him in any way she could. She would not stop now.

"You must rest here tonight, tomorrow we will find Narabius. If that old fool can't help you, then no Shellac can!" Coralada smiled as she spoke, she had known Narabius all of her life. She respected him as a wise elder—but she could also remember many of the foolish decisions he had made when he was younger, ruled by his heart and not by his head.

Willie and Lackey finished their moss-weevil soup, only to be given another bowlful from Coralada. "Eat up you will need all your strength if you are to challenge The Dark Spirit," she said, emptying every last drop from the kettle.

"Never thought insects could taste so good," said Willie, soaking up the last of his soup with the stonebread as he spoke.

After they had finished eating, Coralada led them into a small lounge area.

"Sit yourselves by the fire while I make you a nice hot cup of moss tea," she said as she disappeared back into the kitchen.

"She's a good woman, yer aunt Coralada."

Lackey nodded, "Lackey very proud, to call her 'aunt'."

"Will she know where to find Narabius? Is he here in the caves?" asked Willie.

"Yes, Coralada knows where. Deeper in caves, where water of life touches earth and sky."

Willie looked bemused, "water of life touches the earth and the sky?"

"Yes friend, you will see. Coralada will show us. Willie rest now, we have much to do."

Coralada came back into the room, a mug of moss tea in each hand, "here you are boys, drink up; drink while it's hot. Then sleep, we will leave early in the morning." She handed the mugs of tea to Willie and Lackey before disappearing back into the kitchen.

Lackey and Willie chatted for a while, drinking their tea before both falling sound asleep.

The following morning, Willie was awoken by the sound of a solitary horn being blown, somewhere in the Shellac kingdom. The sound echoed from the stone walls, waking everyone who still slept.

"Willie, Willie, come quickly! Shellac huntsmen returning," shouted Lackey as he rushed to the mouth of their cave.

Willie stood up quickly, banging his head on the stone ceiling above him.

"A-A-A-R-R-G-H, ma heed," he yelled as he rushed to Lackey's side.

Lackey stood in silence as a group of about thirty Shellac huntsmen made their way through the marketplace below them. The huntsmen limped and hobbled along, most of them sporting some kind of injury; several even had to be carried on stretchers. The huntsmen carried deer carcasses, rabbits and mountain hares, four of them carried a huge wild boar between them. They often ventured into the forest for up to five days at a time. hunting for food; wild animals, fruits—anything they could find, including the wild boar that lived right on the edge of the forest. The catch this time, however was much smaller than usual. The huntsmen had been ambushed by Black Hammers. several of them would not be returning, their souls having been claimed for The Dark Spirit. The rumours of the attack began to spread quickly, some saying a hundred or more Black Hammers had been involved. Some of the rumours involved Mudthogs; and even The Dark Spirit himself.

"Willie, we must be on our way," said Lackey as he went back inside the cave.

Coralada was busy at the stove, preparing what looked like rabbit stew.

"Come, sit down. Eat, fill yourselves, then we shall go and find Narabius," she said, placing two bowls of stew onto the table for Willie and Lackey.

They sat and ate the stew in silence; both aware, that if the rumours of the attack on the huntsmen were to be believed, that time was running out. After they had finished eating, Willie gathered his webbing sack and carefully checked its contents. The pixie pogrom was softly cushioned in a towel, his sling resting alongside.

"Time to get going," said Coralada as she collected a pouch of gold coins from a draw in the kitchen, securing them around her waist.

"We must head south, through the silver fern and on to the misty lake, there we should find Narabius—if the old fool hasn't gone and died on us," she said laughing.

They carefully made their way down the criss-cross of walkways, until they reached the marketplace.

Coralada approached one of the vendors, "morning Necious dear, two pairs of your finest moss boots please," she began. "You'd better make one pair extra large," she added, staring at Willie's feet.

Necious took two pairs of moss boots and handed them to Coralada.

"That will be seven gold coins please; I've had to charge one extra due to the oversized pair. You know, the price of good quality moss these days has risen to ten gold coins a thillet."

Coralada nodded as she removed seven gold coins from her pouch and handed them over to Necious.

"Thank you Coralada, you won't find better quality moss boots on the market."

Coralada stuffed the boots into Willie's sack, "you never know when you might need a pair of moss boots; I never go anywhere without mine." She smiled as she spoke, fastening the webbing sack securely.

"Quickly now, we must go, follow Lackey."

They continued through the marketplace, urgency in every step.

"How long until we reach Narabius?" asked Willie as they got closer to the silver ferns.

"Not long, we shall reach him soon," replied Coralada as she was helped along by Lackey.

The huge chasm inside the moss caves, through which they were walking, led them to an area which was densely covered with silver fern. The ceiling in the chasm opened up, exposing a dark morning sky filled with stars which shone brightly above them—like hundreds of torches shining through a thick black blanket.

"Stars in the sky, but it's morning," said Willie staring into the sky above him.

"Remember friend, you in Lethavian's world now, a dark world," replied Lackey as they began to walk through the silver fern, each sprong curled tightly up.

Willie noticed a distinct difference to any silver fern he had ever seen before. "This fern really is silver," he said as he held a piece in his hand.

"Yes Willie, this is silver; silver fern, harvested for its healing powers. It has given new life to many a Shellac huntsman. Treat it with respect and in turn it will guide you through life and beyond," said Coralada, picking several fresh tips and pressing them firmly into Willie's hand.

"Come, we must continue, not far to go now."

Willie found the experience of walking through the silver fern, with stars dancing above him, a calming and peaceful one. He felt safe in the moss caves, the opening above him (into the dark sky) was heavily guarded by Shellac huntsmen.

They did not have to continue for much further before the silver fern gradually faded away as they reached the edge of a mist-covered lake.

A small wooden jetty stretched out from the water's edge, alongside it moored a small rowing boat. They approached the boat, which was occupied by a Shellac boatman.

"Where to?" asked the boatman as he eyed Willie up and down.

"To the water of life please," replied Coralada.

"That will be one gold coin each; make that two for your oversized companion."

Coralada removed four gold coins from her pouch and handed them over to the boatman.

"Right, climb in. I suggest the big fellow sits in the middle, otherwise the only place we'll be going today is round in circles."

Lackey gave a snigger, amused by the boatman's (not so subtle) dig at Willie.

Willie stepped in first, pushing his foot down firmly into the bottom of the boat and causing it to slam against the wooden jetty, sending a wave of water over Lackey.

Willie grinned, "now who's laughing ma wee friend?" he said as he sat down in the boat and helped Coralada aboard.

"Right ma wee soggy friend, ye're next," he said, offering his outstretched hand. Lackey took hold and climbed in.

Once everyone was settled, and the balance in the boat was right, the boatman pushed off from the jetty and started to row.

The boat glided calmly along the water's surface and into the mist.

An eerie silence fell around them, the only sound to be heard was that of the oar breaking the water's surface. The mist seemed to get thicker until nothing at all could be seen. The boatman continued to row, he had crossed the lake so many times that he did not need to see the way, he knew it in his head, his senses guided him along.

The sound of cascading water broke the silence; faintly at first, but steadily increasing in volume as they continued to move through the water. The mist gradually began to lift, Willie could make out the shoreline in the distance. The air began to fill with moisture.

"Darn the rain, looks like we're in for a soaking." Willie held out his hand as drops of water began to bounce from his palm.

"Not rain friend, spray from water of life... look." Lackey pointed over Willie's shoulder.

"Well I'll be!" he exclaimed as he strained his neck to see, not wanting to rock the boat too much, "the water of life," he murmured, as his eyes settled onto a single cascade of water, crashing into the lake just in front of them. Willie slowly ran his eyes up the column of water until he could see no further, the water disappearing into the heavens above them.

"Where the water of life touches the earth and the sky! So we are here? Narabius is here?"

Coralada smiled, "yes Willie, with a bit of luck we should find him here."

The boat came alongside another wooden jetty, the boatman jumped out and secured it tightly.

"Here we are, everybody out," said the boatman as he took Coralada's hand and helped her ashore, quickly followed by Willie and Lackey, relieved to be back on firmer ground.

Willie's eyes remained fixed on the column of water, his common sense doubting, but his eyes believing what he saw.

"Beautiful, isn't it? A single column of water, beginning nowhere and ending nowhere, full of tales and myths—and full of life." Coralada opened her hand to catch some of the spray, rubbing it between her fingers, "Narabius is here, that old fool never ventures far from the water of life."

Coralada pointed to a small opening in the rock face in front of them.

"That opening is his home. Come, follow me." Coralada took Lackey's hand and headed for the opening. As they got closer, a Shellac appeared at the entrance to the opening.

"Coralada, I have been expecting you; and this pair must be Lackey and Willie I presume?"

"Hello Narabius my old friend, nice to see you after all this time." Coralada greeted Narabius with a hug, their friendship had spanned many moon phases and, although she often described him as an 'old fool,' she had utmost loyalty and respect for him.

"Please come inside, we have no time to waste," said Narabius as he headed back through the opening, the others followed close behind.

Narabius led them down a narrow walkway into his home. His single room was carved into the rock; it was sparsely furnished and allowed for little comfort. It was, however, more than adequate for Narabius, who had chosen to live a simple life, going without material things. His wisdom was held deep in his mind, through his experiences and interactions; knowledge itself, his most powerful tool. The only luxury he had was being able to drink from the water of life each morning and each evening.

"You have grown up well Lackey, your parents would have been proud of you. You have done a fine job Coralada."

Narabius's words stirred a mixture of emotion in Lackey.

"We come for help wise one; your help to destroy..."

"Yes I know, The Dark Spirit. I know why you are here Lackey, I have been expecting you—and Willie."

Willie looked surprised, "ye can't have been expecting me, ye don't know me."

"You're right Willie, I don't know you, but I have been following you now for sometime. You, your son Cameron, and his friends Finn and Erin, I have been watching you all."

"Cameron, you know where he is? Is he well?" asked Willie, desperate to hear news of his son.

"Do not worry yourself about Cameron, or his friends. Theodore will look after them. They make good progress towards the inner evildom of The Dark Spirit."

"But how... how can you see them?" asked Willie.

Narabius smiled, pointing to his head, "I see most things; my mind's eye allows me that gift."

Willie sat down on the floor, he knew he was no longer in his own world, but things were still taking time to sink in.

"I knew you were the one to help us, that is why I sent for you."

"*You* sent for *me*, I think yer mistaken Narabius."

"Yes, I sent for you Willie. I sent Lackey to guide you here."

Lackey now also looked confused.

"Lackey stumbled across Willie in the bog, close to the castle."

"Yes Lackey you did, but through my doing. You were hungry, you stole Willie's sack. You said that you didn't mean to do it, did not know what came over you."

"Yes, Lackey not know what came over him."

Narabius started to chuckle, "I came over you Lackey. I—Narabius—made you steal Willie's sack."

Lackey sat down on the floor next to Willie.

"So what now Narabius?" asked Coralada.

"Now, my dear, we advance towards the inner evildom of The Dark Spirit."

"Do you know the way Narabius?" asked Lackey.

"Of course I know the way Lackey; and furthermore, I have gathered together the finest Shellac warriors to have ever stepped foot in our Shellac kingdom. They will guide you on your way, ensuring you a safe passage. Come along we must prepare."

With that Narabius scurried back out of the cave and over to the water of life.

"Follow me, quickly," he said as he went.

As Willie and Lackey stepped out of the cave they were greeted by twelve Shellac warriors.

"So these are the best ye have eh?" said Willie, staring at the fragile-looking creatures in front of him.

"Do not underestimate them Willie; as both power and wisdom come from within," Narabius nodded to one of the warriors as he spoke.

The warrior approached Willie, quickly taking hold of his bushy orange beard, giving it a sharp and painful yank.

"Ouch! ye wee devil, come here," he shouted, lunging at the warrior, "come here!"

But the warrior was too quick. Every time Willie tried to grab him he just seemed to disappear into thin air.

"Wee blighter, I'll have ye yet."

Willie lunged at the warrior once more, but before he had time to get to him the warrior lifted Willie clean off his feet and threw him; like a rag doll, into the lake. Coughing and spluttering, Willie burst through the surface of the water.

"Ok ye made yer point!"

Lackey rolled around on the water's edge, laughing uncontrollably as Willie heaved himself back onto dry land.

"My warriors will lead you to the inner evildom of The Dark Spirit; and I shall be following your progress closely. Once inside, you must destroy The Dark Spirit, part him from the Purple Crystal. I will be of little use to you once inside Lethavian's domain; my mind's eye has no vision in there. I will, however, guide you as best I can up until that time. My warriors will give you protection and loyal service. In return, treat them with the respect they rightly deserve."

Willie dropped his head, embarrassed for previously doubting the Shellac warriors' abilities.

"Before you go, drink from the water of life. It will rejuvenate you and keep you strong," said Narabius, still amused by Willie.

Lackey, Willie and the twelve Shellac warriors, drank from the water. It tasted good and gave them all a sense of wellbeing.

"Take care Lackey dear, may you return to us safely," said Coralada as she hugged her adopted son, tears in her eyes.

"Same goes for you Willie, the Shellac will be forever grateful to you, as will your own kind," said Narabius as he shook Willie's hand firmly.

Willie and Lackey were now led by the Shellac warriors as they started to climb the moss caves. Weaving along narrow walkways, they got closer to the opening, in the ceiling, of the huge chasm.

After a short while they reached the top, pausing momentarily as the water of life cascaded down next to them. The stars above them shone brightly in the black sky as they stepped out of the Shellac kingdom and began the descent into the Black Forest below.

Chapter 9

THE MISSING PAGE

The black moon cast an array of shadows across the ground as Cameron, Erin, Finn and Theodore stepped from the Ocean Room and into the open air.

The smell of the heather warmed Cameron's heart, but he had a strange feeling in the pit of his stomach; a strange, yet not unpleasant, feeling. He knew the feeling was for his father, who he was sure continued to breathe the same air as him.

"Where are we, Theodore?" asked Erin as she studied the surrounding area.

"We're in the open, my first time in many years. The cool air on my face and the smell of the bell heather allow me that knowledge, as for the name of this place, I know it not."

"Perhaps we are in the Black Forest, just like the speaking books told us; perhaps the page was ripped out because nothing exists between the Ocean Room and the Black Forest." Finn felt a rush of excitement racing through his body as he spoke, believing that they might now be closer to The Dark Spirit than he had previously thought.

"Can you smell that? Freshly baked bread, and—" Erin sniffed the air as she spoke, "bacon. Yes, I can definitely smell bacon." Erin smiled as the satisfying aromas wafted through her nostrils.

Cameron regarded Erin with puzzlement, he too sniffing the air.

"I think you're dreaming; the only thing I can smell is the bell heather, nothing more."

Erin looked confused, "but you must smell it, it's so strong. Finn, Theodore, surely you must smell the bread and the bacon?"

"I can smell something, but it's not bacon. Smells more like a Sunday roast to me," replied Finn

"I, like Cameron, only smell the heather, the most beautiful heather I have smelt in a long time. I think we need to rest, your minds are obviously playing tricks on you." Theodore smiled, chuckling to himself as he spoke. "Bacon indeed, the chance would be a fine thing."

The four friends sat a while under a large oak tree, their conversation focusing on the whereabouts of Willie and Lackey.

"I know they're alive; father deliberately dropped his tartan scarf as a sign, I know he did." Cameron spoke happily about his father, and how he was sure that they would all meet up again very soon.

They ate the last remaining morsels of food from Cameron's rucksack before each of them fell fast asleep; all that was, except Theodore. He remained alert, listening to the wind as it gently blew through the trees.

****

"Wake! We must hurry on, time is not on our side," Theodore placed his hand on the sleeping body next to him and shook it.

"OK, OK I'm awake," said Finn as he reluctantly sat up, stretching his arms above his head.

Cameron and Erin also awoke, somewhat dazed from the deep sleep they had fallen into, but ready to continue.

"How long have we been asleep?" asked Erin as she wiped the sleep from her eyes.

"I'm not sure my child, time is difficult to measure in this world of perpetual darkness," replied Theodore as he stood to his feet. "I only know that time is silently passing us by."

The four friends then set off into the forest; none of them sure of exactly where they were heading, but all feeling an overwhelming confidence that it was in the right direction.

"Father!" exclaimed Cameron as he froze to the spot. "Father, is that you?"

Finn and Erin peered into the darkness, following Cameron's gaze, hoping to see what had provoked his outburst. Despite their best efforts, all they saw was shadow, dancing around the gnarled tree trunks and dense undergrowth.

"I can't see anyone. Where are you looking, Cameron?" asked Finn. Cameron remained silent, desperately trying to catch another glimpse of Willie.

"There, look! Father, over here, OVER HERE!" Cameron's words were caught up in the breeze that blew through the forest and were carried off into the distance. He stood motionless, listening, waiting for a response. None came.

"Blast, he didn't hear me. But it *was* him, I knew he was alive! Come on, we must follow him; he looked like he was in a hurry, he must know the way."

Cameron quickly set off in the direction he was sure he'd seen Willie.

"Wait Cameron, are you sure it was Willie you saw?" asked Finn, not wanting to make a hasty decision that they may later regret.

"Call me a liar do you? of course it was Willie, stupid; I *can* recognise my own father." Cameron's reply was short and abrupt; he had thought Finn trusted his decisions, but that was obviously not the case.

'I only asked' thought Finn, not wanting to reply verbally and make the situation any worse.

Cameron turned and set off into the forest, not wanting to waste any more time.

"Don't be too hard on the boy," said Theodore. "Not knowing whether his father was dead or alive must have been difficult for him to deal with."

"You're right, Theodore. We must support him just as he has supported us," said Erin as she took Theodore's hand in her left and Finn's hand in her right, giving both a squeeze.

"Come on, let's follow him before we loose sight of him," said Finn, quickly setting off after Cameron.

"Lead the way child," said Theodore, holding tightly to Erin's hand as they set off to follow both Cameron and Finn.

All three soon managed to catch up with Cameron as he huffed and puffed along. He had never been an athletic child, although his size and strength more than compensated for his lack of speed and stamina.

"Have you seen him again?" asked Finn.

Cameron did not answer, instead he simply shook his head, his sadness was obvious.

"Sorry for being a bit snappy, but it was definitely my father I saw—and Lackey. They're both still alive and both still together." Cameron smiled, he felt as if a great burden had been lifted from his shoulders now that he knew his father was still alive.

The hairs on the back of Erin's neck stood on end as she spun around to look deep into the forest. She sensed a thousand eyes staring at her, burning into her skin like hot pokers.

"What is it, child?" asked Theodore as he felt her grip on his hand tighten.

"I'm not sure *what* it is, but I can sense someone—or something -watching us. I can feel whoever it is watching us now."

"Don't be stupid, Erin," said Cameron abruptly. "Nobody is watching you, or us; we are alone in the forest."

Erin scowled as she stared directly at Cameron.

"Stupid am I? Well just because I'm the only one that can sense it, doesn't make me stupid. After all, you're the only one who claims to have seen Willie; so what does that make you?" said Erin, sneering as she spoke.

"We must stop all this bickering. To succeed we must work together, not against each other." Theodore hoped his words would bring unity back to the group.

"I'm sorry, Cameron. I don't know why I spoke to you like that," said Erin, hanging her head and clearly a little ashamed of herself.

"I'm sorry too, I didn't mean to doubt you." Cameron stretched out his hand as he spoke.

"Together. We work together," replied Erin as she grabbed hold of Cameron's hand, happy to be friends again.

A Black Hammer swooped low over their heads, its evil yellow eyes absorbing information as it passed. It then flew off, out of sight.

"Did you see that?" asked Finn, hoping not to have been the only one to have seen the bird.

"The Black Hammer? yes I saw it," replied Cameron.

"Me too," said Erin.

"Then he knows we are here, his eyes have spotted us. We must continue—quickly." Theodore stroked his beard, concerned that their location had been revealed to Lethavian.

"But I don't know which way to go; I've lost track of my father," said Cameron, now worried for the safety of them all.

"Go with your feelings, let them be your guide," urged Theodore, keen for them to quickly get back on their way.

"That way!" said Cameron, Finn, and Erin, in unison, all pointing in the same direction. It was as if the thought had flashed into their heads at exactly the same moment.

"WOW, I knew the twin thing was spooky—but triplets?" Cameron laughed out loud, amused by their synchronized thinking.

"Then let us go before *he* spots us again," said Theodore, pleased that a decision had been made without any falling out.

The forest fell silent as the four friends continued to travel through it, driven on by their thoughts of capturing the Purple

Crystal and destroying The Dark Spirit. Such was their determination to succeed and the focus on the task in hand, they were completely unaware that they were being followed.

As they hurried along, the shadows began to move; changing shape and direction. They grew, like balloons being inflated; then, just as quickly, they disappeared. They stretched and then shrank; twisted, then contorted. Some of the shadows looked vaguely human and appeared to be running through the forest, turning their heads to stare at the four friends as they went.

"This place is giving me the creeps, I hope we're going the right way." Erin sounded both frightened and concerned as she spoke. She tried to focus her gaze directly ahead—as though wearing blinkers—in an attempt to block all trace of the shadows from her view.

"Have faith in yourself, Erin; for shadows are merely, and no more than, an obstruction of light." Theodore's words reassured her as she struggled to keep up with Cameron and Finn, who were just ahead.

****

Black Hammers began to fill the sky, silently gliding through the air; listening, watching, and feeding their information back to The Dark Spirit. The evil birds focused their attention on the four friends as they continued on their journey.

****

The shadows continued to torment Erin, who maintained her tight grip on Theodore's hand as they followed Cameron and Finn. All four were unaware that an army of Black Hammers were mustering in the sky, just out of their view. Thousands of birds from all four corners of Lethavian's evil kingdom had congregated, preparing to attack.

The four friends had been travelling now for some time, still unsure of their direction and not just a little disheartened by the knowledge that they might actually be heading further away from The Dark Spirit.

"Stop! Cameron, Finn, I need to rest," Erin shouted ahead. Her legs ached and she needed to sit a while to regain her strength.

"We can't stop for long, we must be getting close," said Finn as he sat down next to his sister.

"Close? Close to what?" Erin snapped back at Finn, annoyed by his unfounded comment.

"Don't shout at me! If you can't keep up then you can stay here, I really don't care."

Finn's words cut through Erin like a knife, she could not understand why he was being so nasty to her.

"Shut up! Both of you shut up, or I'll leave you both here," shouted Cameron, at Finn and Erin. "You're just holding me up anyway, I never asked you to come along."

The four sat, resting and totally silent, not even wanting to look at each other for fear of reprisal. Theodore was stroking his beard again, something he did a lot when trying to concentrate.

"Right, I've had enough. Are we just going to sit here all day, or are we going to get what we came for?" asked Cameron, jumping back to his feet.

Just as Finn was about to answer, something in the sky above them caught his eye. As he turned his head to glance upward, he saw hundreds of Black Hammers swooping down toward them.

"Watch out, we're under attack, RUN! RUN!"

By the time the words had found their way out of his mouth, the first of the Black Hammers had reached them and a frenzy of activity had begun.

Erin screamed as she waved her arms about, desperately trying to fight off the feathered vermin. Finn and Cameron also thrashed about frantically to fend off the evil birds.

Talons and beaks nipped and stung as they ripped through clothing and into flesh.

The Black Hammers continued to attack, showing no signs of stopping. The evil birds continued their merciless attack until all four had lost sight of one another, having become engulfed in black feathers, flapping wings and evil yellow eyes.

Injured and disorientated, Cameron, Finn and Erin continued to fight off the birds. Their arms received the worst of the attack as they desperately tried to shield their faces.

A biting wind started to blow through the forest. It appeared from nowhere, acting like a sign to the Black Hammers to retreat.

The birds once more took to the air, as if called away by a voice which only they could hear. Slowly, they made their way off into the distance. Like a thunderous cloud passing through the heavens, the birds vanished from sight as quickly as they had appeared; leaving their prey weak and confused, nursing their wounds on the ground below.

The cold wind that blew through the forest had disappeared at almost the same time that the Black Hammers flew off, leaving a deathly silence. Cameron, Erin and Finn lay dazed and confused on the ground, speechless after the attack they had just experienced; each one of them in total shock, but relieved to be alive.

"Finn, Erin, are you alright?" enquired Cameron, as he lay motionless on the ground.

"I'm OK, but my arms are cut," said Erin shakily.

"I'm OK too, a bit grazed though," mumbled Finn.

"Theodore, what about you? Are you OK?" asked Cameron. He waited for his companion's reply, but it did not come.

"THEODORE!" shouted Erin, sitting upright to look around. "Theodore, can you hear me?"

The three friends desperately waited for an answer, but the forest fell into silence once more. Theodore was gone.

"Come on, we must find him. He must be here somewhere." Erin's words were edged with panic as she frantically began to search for Theodore.

Cameron and Finn joined Erin in the search, but Theodore was nowhere to be seen.

"It's no good, he's not here; we must stop now," said Cameron, saddened by their loss, yet still focused on the Purple Crystal.

"If we don't stop looking now, we will only get ourselves even more confused. We won't know which way we are going, or which way we have come. Theodore has gone but we must continue."

Erin collapsed with nervous exhaustion, overwhelmed by the situation she was now facing.

"Come on sister, Cameron is right," said Finn as he went over to where Erin was kneeling to help her to her feet.

"Gosh, the cuts on your arms are deep. They need cleaning," Finn's words were full of genuine concern for his sister.

The Black Hammers had definitely left their mark. Her cuts and grazes were far worse than anything that had been inflicted on either Cameron or Finn. Cameron removed his flask from his rucksack. He also removed the handkerchief from his pocket and shook the last remaining mints from it onto the forest floor. He soaked the handkerchief with the water from the flask.

"Finn, carefully roll her sleeves up," instructed Cameron, before he gently bathed Erin's arms.

"OUCH! That stings," said Erin, starting to cry.

"Don't worry, Erin. You're going to be just fine, I promised you didn't I?" Erin nodded at Cameron, he had promised to protect her and she felt sure he would do just that.

'If only my father was here, he would know what to do,' thought Cameron as he tore Willie's tartan scarf into strips and used them as bandages to dress Erin's wounds, to keep dirt and infection out and to help stem the bleeding.

"What do you think happened to Theodore?" asked Erin, tears

welling in her eyes.

"I don't know, I lost sight of everyone during the attack. Perhaps the Black Hammers took him," replied Cameron.

"He saved my life in the firing gallery and now he's gone," sobbed Erin uncontrollably.

"Shhh—don't upset yourself. I'm sure that canny old man will give those Black Hammers a run for their money," said Cameron as he placed his arms around her to give her some comfort.

"We must go; we must go and get the Purple Crystal and destroy The Dark Spirit; for Theodore. We owe him at least that much," said Finn as he stood up and walked across to Erin, to help her to her feet.

Weakened but not defeated, the three friends supported each other as they continued on their mission.

****

Aware that the commotion from the Black Hammer attack had now stopped, Willie looked upwards and saw the cloud of Black Hammers, as they flew off into the distance; a wry smile spread across his face. He was even more determined to catch up with Cameron and his friends, who were now just a short distance ahead.

****

The three friends moved slowly. The exertion of defending themselves against the Black Hammers had weakened them all. They were sore, bruised and tired, but remained focused on the Purple Crystal and the slim hope of seeing Theodore, Willie and Lackey again.

Willie and Lackey now had the three weary friends in sight. Willie felt a surge of excitement flood through his body. The excitement was like that experienced by a hunter as he closed in on his prey.

"Come ma wee friend, we'll nip round in front o' them, give 'em a right surprise we will," he said with eyes bulging with desire. Willie took hold of Lackey's hand and started to skirt widely around Cameron, Finn and Erin, so that he could meet them head on.

****

"Look, over there," said Cameron pointing into the forest. "Father? Is that you? It's me Cameron, I'm over here."

Willie did not reply but disappeared quickly from sight.

"I saw him too," said Finn. "That mass of orange hair is unmistakable."

"Why didn't he answer? He must have heard me shouting!"

Cameron looked puzzled, he could not understand why his father had ignored him.

"Come on, let's keep going. If that *was* Willie, then at least we're all heading in the same direction."

Finn's words encouraged the others to keep going, reassuring them that they were, in fact, heading the right way.

After only a short while the forest began to thin out and the dense undergrowth started to give way to areas of open land.

"This must be the edge of the forest, we must be nearly there." Erin's tired face broke into a smile, finding the energy from somewhere as she plodded wearily along.

"FATHER," shouted Cameron.

"WILLIE! LACKEY! IS THAT YOU?" Finn shouted. All three stood perfectly still, staring ahead into the area of open land.

Willie and Lackey were standing in the centre of the clearing, waving to the three friends.

"I knew they were alive, I knew it," said Cameron as his eyes filled with emotion; clearly relieved to see his father again.

"I'm sorry I doubted you, Cameron. Of course you saw Willie in the forest," said Finn, feeling bad for having previously questioned his friend. As the three children approached Willie they saw his rosy cheeks and a smile, so big, it almost split his face in two.

"Hello son, thought I'd surprise ye," he said, stretching out his arms as Cameron ran to greet him.

An intense pain shot through Erin's head; a blinding pain which came from nowhere, forcing her to drop to her knees. She closed her eyes and her face became contorted in agony as she buried her head deep into her hands. The pain then disappeared, just as quickly as it had arrived. Erin's eyes remained shut tight as... an image of Theodore appeared in her mind. The image was quite clear and, unmistakably, one of Theodore. He seemed to be talking to her, repeating the name of Lethavian over and over. With her head still in her hands, Erin opened her eyes and peered through the gaps between her fingers. Her gaze landed on the red tartan scarf used by Cameron to bandage her arms. She then glanced ahead, to where Willie stood with Lackey, beckoning Cameron to them.

Erin's contorted face turned to one of shock and, disbelief. "Cameron stop! Please stop, that isn't Willie. THAT ISN'T YOUR FATHER," screamed Erin. "Look at his scarf!"

Cameron slowed down, his beaming smile reduced to a bitter and sad frown.

"Father," he said, looking at Willie, obviously confused.

"That isn't Willie, Cameron. Don't let him fool you. Look at him!

How can he be wearing the scarf that you used to bandage my arms. The very same one that you're wearing now, over your shoulder."

Willie stood in silence, a flowing red scarf draped over his huge body. Willie then started to laugh, but it was not Willie's voice. It was a painful and twisted laugh, one which sent shivers running down Cameron's spine.

The three friends turned to run, but found themselves surrounded by hundreds of Mudthogs.

Turning back to face where Willie had stood, they now saw the figure of a man dressed entirely in black, a hood covering his face and a Purple Crystal hanging from a chain around his neck.

"It's him! I recognise him! That's the man that tried to strangle me in the forest. The Dark Spirit." Finn's words left both Cameron and Erin breathless and unable to reply.

The Mudthogs started to close in on them; they were completely surrounded with nowhere to run.

Anger welled up inside Cameron, he had been made to look a fool. His friend had been taken by the Black Hammers, but much worse The Dark Spirit had used the likeness of his own father to torment him.

"YOU EVIL BEAST!," he screamed, finding his voice as he rushed towards The Dark Spirit.

The painful and twisted tone continued to fill the air as Lethavian stood laughing at them.

Cameron lunged at Lethavian, determined to capture the Purple Crystal and to destroy him. Just as he felt his hands making contact, The Dark Spirit vanished into thin air, his laugh slowly echoing into the distance.

The Mudthogs were now just feet away, all holding swords aloft, ready to attack.

The army of Black Hammers returned to the sky above them. The mass of birds blocked the glow given off by the moon, their shadow casting the three friends into almost total darkness. The Black Hammers dived towards them and the flurry of activity began anew. Talons and beaks ripped into flesh and bone. The Mudthogs began to rain blow after blow upon them; the dark cold metal of their swords slicing effortlessly through arms and legs until finally, Cameron, Erin and Finn allowed the final gasps of air to depart their bodies.

The forest fell into silence as the Black Hammers returned to the sky and flew off into the distance. The Mudthogs disappeared back into the darkness of the dense undergrowth. Cameron, Erin and Finn lay motionless on the ground. The smell of the forest floor was one of rot and decay as the life drained from shrubs, and trees alike. The air became moist as a fine drizzle descended from the sky above. Cameron's eye flickered as the rain touched his face and ran down his cheek. He was still alive!

****

"Wake up! Wake up! Cameron, Finn, Erin, wake up!" said Theodore as he frantically shook at the three sleeping bodies, splashing water from Cameron's flask over them.

"Wake up! You have slept long enough, we must go."

Slowly, all three started to wake; their brows drenched in sweat, and burn water. Erin swung her arms around in the air, as if fighting off an invisible attacker. Cameron sat bolt-upright, pale with fear.

"Where is he? Where is The Dark Spirit?"

Theodore smiled, "he is not here my child; there are only the four of us."

Finn opened his eyes, dazed and confused, "where are we?" he asked, glancing around.

"We are in the same place you fell asleep not ten minutes ago, under the oak tree; just outside of the Ocean Room," replied Theodore.

Erin opened her eyes, "Theodore, I thought you were dead, I thought the Black Hammers had claimed your soul," she said, wrapping her arms around his neck.

"Don't worry child, you're quite safe. You're *all* quite safe," said Theodore happy to have his friends back.

"You now know the mystery of the missing page."

Cameron, Finn and Erin looked confused at Theodore's words.

"What do you mean?" asked Finn, still reeling from the shock of what he thought had just happened to him.

"The page was ripped out of my speaking book because nothing exists between the Ocean Room and the Black Forest, you were right Finn; nothing exists. Everything that you have just experienced, everything that has just happened to you, happened only in your mind."

Theodore's words left the three friends shocked and even more confused.

Erin looked at her arms, no longer bound with Willie's red tartan scarf, completely unblemished; not even a small scratch visible.

"I knew something was wrong when I couldn't wake you. That's why I had to look into your mind, Erin. Remember?" said Theodore.

Erin thought for a moment. "Yes, I remember. A blinding pain in my head and then I saw you. I saw you, Theodore, in my mind; you were warning us."

Theodore placed his arms around her. "Yes child and you did well. Once The Dark Spirit had left your thoughts I was able to bring you back, to wake you from your torment."

"My father? Does Lethavian control *him?* Has he claimed *his* soul?" asked Cameron as he stood to his feet.

"Worry not, child. Your father is still alive; alive and well. I saw that much in Lethavian's eyes as I stared at him through your mind, Willie and Lackey continue with our quest."

Theodore's words reassured the group.

"Then we must continue—we have time to make up," said Finn as he also got to his feet, at Cameron's side.

The four friends gathered themselves and set off into the Black Forest. The aromas of bread, bacon, Sunday roast and bell heather had gone—yet another game played by Lethavian. The only smell that remained was that of the damp forest floor.

Chapter 10

TWO SIDES OF ONE COIN

The four friends soon found themselves surrounded by shrubs, trees, and vines from the heavily-covered undergrowth of the Black Forest. They made good progress, even though they were not really sure where they were heading.

Before very long, Cameron began to have doubts as to whether he was actually *in* the Black Forest, or was he still dreaming? His mind still under the power of The Dark Spirit. Every now and then he would glance, unexpectedly, this way and that way—each time hoping to catch a glimpse of his father—but each time he was left feeling disappointed.

A solitary Black Hammer followed their progress, soaring high above them so as not to be spotted. Theodore alone was aware that they were being followed, he saw the Black Hammer in his mind's eye, the vision was accompanied by the knowledge that he was been watched by his own brother. He did not want to alarm his three friends, so he said nothing, aware that the images and feelings of previous events were still very much on their minds.

"How much further, Theodore?" asked a weary Erin.

"As far as is necessary for the completion of our task," said Theodore, smiling, fully aware that his response was vague, even if it was as accurate an answer as he could give.

The dense forest tested their physical abilities to the limit. It twisted and turned like an obstacle course, slowing their progress and leading them in whatever direction it chose.

After several more minutes, the forest led them to the edge of a large lake. The dense undergrowth gave way to a shoreline of sandy-brown pebbles, smoothed by the action of the dark blue water as it lapped over them.

"Where are we?" asked Finn as he looked around, absorbing information.

"I'm not sure, a huge lake somewhere in the forest; so calm and tranquil, a beautiful sight," said Cameron, breathing in deeply through his nostrils. "The air smells so fresh."

"A perfect place to rest a while," said Theodore as he sat on the pebbles and stretched out his legs.

"Was that really The Dark Spirit in our minds, Theodore?" asked Erin, still visibly shaken by the ordeal of having her thoughts controlled by someone else.

"Yes, child. Lethavian is very strong, his powers constantly pushing the boundaries. He was able to play with all your minds at the same time, even allowing your thought processes to interact with one another."

As Theodore spoke he heard a sound, somewhere in the distance; past, future, or present distance he did not know. He was aware that he alone had heard the sound, it was the sound of Lethavian's voice.

"Theodore, are you alright? Your face has gone really white," asked Erin, looking concerned for her friend.

"Yes child, I am fine. My mind is active, that's all."

Theodore heard the familiar sound of his brother's voice again, repeatedly calling out his name, "Theodore, Theodore, Theodore."

The voice then began to laugh, causing a painful stabbing feeling in Theodore's chest. Theodore hated his brother, hated him for what he had done to his own family, and for the pain and misery he continued to inflict on others. He sat stroking his long white beard, *'Why is Lethavian calling to me? Why, after all this time does he choose to speak to me?'* Theodore pondered his brother's intentions, he knew that soon they would meet again, after many long years of separation.

Cameron, Erin and Finn now stood at the water's edge, skimming pebbles across its surface. The air was filled with the sound of their laughter as they relaxed for a while and even enjoyed themselves. Theodore smiled to himself, the sound of their laughter warmed his heart.

"Theodore, Theodore," Lethavian's voice, found its way to Theodore, as if planted into his brain by some kind of telepathy, between brothers. Theodore stood to his feet and wondered back into the forest, his brother's words summoned him, leading him away from his three young friends who continued to play at the water's edge, oblivious to anything else that was happening.

"Theodore, Theodore," Lethavian continued to call to his brother, beckoning him, deeper into the forest and further from his three friends. Lethavian's words guided Theodore along, weaving in and out of trees, over rocks and through shrubs, all the time Lethavian's voice became clearer and more sinister.

"Theodore, Theodore brother, come to me."

Theodore found himself unable to do anything, but follow Lethavian's words. His free will had been stripped from him.

Theodore was led into a small opening, deep inside the dense undergrowth. He could feel the ground becoming boggy underfoot and a smell of stale breath hung in the air. He knew Lethavian was close.

"Make yourself known to me, Lethavian. I know you are here," Theodore spoke with authority; he had never feared his brother before and this was definitely not the time to start.

A sound caught his attention. It was the sound of hooves tramping through the muddy undergrowth towards him, he could hear the sucking sound made each time a hoof was pulled out of the mud.

Theodore stood in silence as a black horse, at least twenty hands tall, came to a halt just in front of him. Its nostrils flared as it breathed, sending streams of warm breath spiralling into the damp cool air of the forest.

"So we meet again little brother," Lethavian laughed loudly as he spoke; a laugh which echoed through the forest, like the roaring boom of thunder.

Theodore looked up to his brother's face, toward the source of laughter. Lethavian now sat just inches from him, high on the back of his black charger.

"I see you have not changed, brother. You are still the overbearing, arrogant child you always were. Although, I must admit, you do smell a little sweeter, or is that the horse I smell?" Theodore smirked as he spoke, pleased that even under duress he still retained his sense of humour.

Lethavian continued to laugh, "Yes brother, the smell of power is indeed sweet," he said as he dismounted to stand directly in front of Theodore.

Lethavian, unlike Theodore, stood about six feet tall. His head and face were covered by a veil of black cloth; the only visible part of him was his hands. He had long bony fingers which were tipped with overgrown and discoloured nails, the little finger from his right hand was missing. It was a self-inflicted wound, suffered many moons before when it had been severed as an offering to evil. All that remained was a scar where it had once been; a reminder to all of Lethavian's chosen path, in life as well as in death. Around his neck hung the Purple Crystal which protected him from others and boosted his own power.

"Why now, Lethavian? Why now, after all this time, do you choose to speak with me?" asked Theodore.

Lethavian lifted his hands to his head and lowered his hood, exposing his face. He looked evil, with pale skin and sunken black eyes. His teeth were yellow and rotten. He had little hair on his head, but wore a small, twisted, grey beard on his chin.

"Because I can, brother. Because I can," replied Lethavian.

Theodore turned to walk away but could not, his feet were fixed to the spot as if they had been nailed down.

"You go when I say, brother." Lethavian's voice sounded more menacing than Theodore had ever heard it before.

"You sound worried Lethavian; and so you should be!" exclaimed Theodore, not allowing his brother to unnerve him.

Lethavian lifted his hand and slapped his brother across the cheek. Theodore was unable to do anything but receive the blow gracefully.

"Do not insult me, Theodore. Neither you, nor any of your friends, worries me. But I, I, should be of immense worry to you, and to them. Have you forgotten, little brother? We are one and the same; two sides of one coin; neither of us can survive without the other."

Theodore remained silent as Lethavian started to laugh once more, "oh dear little brother, you haven't told them have you? Told them that Lethavian and Theodore Ping are, in fact, one and the same?" Lethavian continued to laugh; the sound cut into Theodore like a knife being plunged into his stomach, twisting and turning as it went.

"We may have the same blood pumping through our veins—but *that*, Lethavian, is where any resemblance between us stops." Theodore felt anger welling inside him, he would not let Lethavian control him; he would rather die than allow that to happen.

"Do not struggle, brother. You *will* do as I say. You *will* bring me your three friends—so that I can destroy them! As I unleash my power over their world I will let them see hell itself. They will see my power, taste my power, and then die from my power. The three young fools will see who they have chosen to mess with."

Lethavian continued to laugh as Theodore dropped to his knees, weakened by the hold over him.

"You can mess with my mind, Lethavian, but you will not break my spirit, nor claim my soul." Theodore struggled to maintain command of his thoughts, just as Lethavian fought to gain control over them.

"Your mind is strong, brother. Fed of course by mine; you see now, brother, like I said, we are one and the same. Soon we shall combine our efforts and I will control this world."

"Never. I shall never side with you, Lethavian; even in death you will not have me."

"What will it take to change your mind brother? Your eyesight, perhaps?" Lethavian released a surge of energy from his hand which struck Theodore's face, like a fork of lightening.

Theodore steadied himself before slowly opening his eyes. For the first time in many years he could see!

"Time has not been kind to you Lethavian; you look every bit as twisted as you sound. If you think you need to bribe me, brother, then you must be worried," he said as he struggled to muster every last remaining ounce of strength in his body. He lifted his hand to Lethavian, sending a bolt of energy—like an electric current—shooting into Lethavian's right shoulder. The bolt of energy knocked Lethavian backwards, unbalancing him.

He steadied himself, grinning at Theodore. "Good brother, get angry; get really angry; show me your dark side."

"I have no dark side, Lethavian. Only pity; pity for you. You have spent your whole life worshiping evil, amassing your power. I will enjoy reducing you to nothing so much," said Theodore, diving towards his brother, arms outstretched, hoping to grab the Purple Crystal which he could now see hanging around Lethavian's neck.

Lethavian effortlessly brushed off his brother's attack and Theodore fell to the ground at his feet.

"Brother, save your energy. You will need every ounce of it—very soon. The Purple Crystal will remain with me forever, I have become quite attached to it," Lethavian laughed again as he spoke. Again Theodore felt the stabbing pain in his stomach.

"You laugh a lot, Lethavian, for one who will soon take their last breath," Theodore remained at his brother's feet as he spoke.

Lethavian bent down and took hold of Theodore around the neck.

"Do as I say, brother. Bring me those meddling children; bring them to my private quarters.

"Never," replied Theodore.

"Then you leave me with no option," said Lethavian as he

grabbed a webbing sack from the back of his horse and, with all his strength, stuffed a weakened Theodore inside it.

" I have a little surprise for your friends," he taunted. He then proceeded to toss the sack with Theodore inside over the back of his sturdy charger.

"You will find the way, brother. I will be waiting and watching," were the last muffled words Theodore heard before slipping into unconsciousness.

Lethavian turned and remounted his horse.

"Remember brother, we are the two sides of one coin," he shouted to Theodore as he rode off into the forest, his prize firmly secured.

****

Cameron, Erin and Finn continued to play by the water's edge, skimming stones and splashing one another, unaware of the events taking place deep in the forest.

A solitary figure caught their eyes as it emerged from the forest, riding a black horse. The figure, dressed entirely in black, rode the horse across the surface of the lake, a large sack was draped unevenly across the horse's back. Cameron suggested it was carrying the spoils of a hunting trip. Whatever the case, it... left a wake of bubbling black froth as it went. The figure galloped across the lake, into the distance and out of sight. The ripples from the wake lapped onto the shore at the water's edge where the children were playing.

"Wow! What was that?" asked Erin, awestruck at what she had just seen. "You did see it, didn't you? It wasn't just me?" she asked, doubting her own eyes.

"Yes, I saw it. A horse galloping across the surface of the lake, carrying a hooded figure," Cameron's eyes were almost popping out of his head as he spoke, a look of total disbelief etched on his face.

"Theodore, a horse has just galloped across the lake carrying someone on its back," said Erin, turning to where Theodore had sat down to stretch his legs.

"Theodore, where are you?" she said, glancing up and down the shoreline, looking for him.

"Finn; Cameron; Theodore has gone."

The three friends searched frantically around the water's edge and into the forest. They began to panic.

"Theodore, where are you?" shouted Erin, not believing that he would have just walked away and left them without saying a word.

"Theodore, can you hear me? It's me, Finn."

The three friends listened, waiting for a response, but the only sound to be heard was the sound of the wind, gently blowing through the trees.

"He can't have gone far, let's start looking for him," said Cameron, taking control of the situation.

The three friends started to retrace their steps, back into the forest, looking for signs of Theodore.

"I do hope he's alright," said Erin, who had become quite attached to the friendly old man who had certainly saved *her* life on more than one occasion.

"Don't worry, it would take more than Lethavian to claim Theodore's soul." Finn placed a reassuring arm around his sister as he spoke.

"Theodore, can you hear us? Theodore.... THEODORE!" Cameron continued to shout, desperate to alert Theodore to their whereabouts.

"Look! Over there—I see something," said Finn, pointing to a thorny bush.

The three friends walked over to the bush; Erin bent down and picked up a piece of purple cloth with a large yellow jewel attached to it.

"It's a piece of Theodore's cassock; he must have ripped it on the thorns as he passed." Erin's eyes filled with tears, she was happy to have found something of Theodore's, but sad that her friend had gone. She hoped that she was getting closer to him—and that he was still alive.

The three friends pressed on further into the forest, past the thorn bush and over a large mound of rocks and shrubs. They were somehow led into the very opening where Theodore lay, motionless, on the ground.

"Theodore," shouted Erin as she ran over and dropped to one knee, at his side. "Theodore, can you hear me?" she asked, gently stroking his cheek.

"Yes child, I hear you. I was just enjoying the peace and quiet of the forest," he turned to her and smiled.

"Thank goodness you're alright," Erin hugged her friend tightly, relieved to have found him safe and well.

"Theodore, what happened?" asked Cameron as he knelt beside Erin.

"Nothing for you to worry yourselves about, children. let's just say I had an appointment—one which was well overdue."

Finn and Cameron helped Theodore to his feet and the four of them slowly made their way back to the edge of the lake.

"Why didn't you tell us you were going, Theodore? We would have gone with you," asked Erin as she helped him to sit back down on the pebbles.

"I could not my child, he wanted me alone."

"Who wanted you?" she asked, keen to discover who Theodore was talking about.

"My brother," Theodore's reply stopped the conversation dead. The three friends could do no more than stare at him.

"You've seen Lethavian?" asked Cameron, finding his voice at last.

"Yes, child. After all this time, I have spoken with him."

"What did he say?" asked Finn, joining the conversation.

"Something.... and nothing. He merely tried to warn us off; a warning which I treated with the contempt it deserved." Theodore smiled reassuringly, aware that what they had already endured was nothing—compared to what lay ahead.

"The hooded figure on the black horse—that was him? That was The Dark Spirit?" Cameron felt great anger and frustration as he spoke; he loathed The Dark Spirit—more than he had ever loathed anything.

"*You* have seen him?" asked Theodore.

"Yes; he emerged from the forest on the back of a black horse. He galloped across the surface of the lake and disappeared from sight as he rode off into the distance." Finn replied, pointing in the direction that Lethavian had taken.

Theodore chuckled to himself, "if you are pointing in the direction that Lethavian travelled, then hold that image in your mind child, for I cannot see!"

Finn blushed, he hanged his head in embarrassment and stared at his feet. "Sorry, Theodore. I forgot."

Theodore smiled, "our only hope is to follow him," he replied.

"How can we follow him—we don't have a boat....or any other means of following him across the lake for that matter?" said Erin.

Theodore stood up. "Take me to the water's edge, child. Let me feel the water between my toes," he said, stretching out his arm. Erin took hold of his hand and led him to the water's edge.

"Do not be alarmed," Theodore smiled as he lifted both of his arms above his head, "liquidous, fillious, deliverous," he shouted at the water.

At first, nothing seemed to happen. Then, suddenly, the water in the centre of the lake began to bubble violently and a wave of turbulent water began making its way towards them.

"What on earth—or wherever we are—is that?" asked Erin as the bubbling mass of water approached them.

"Our transport; to take us to the far side of the lake," replied Theodore, grinning so widely that Erin feared his face would be split in two.

Upon reaching the shoreline the bubbling water erupted in front of them, covering them all with a fine spray and filling the air. As the spray cleared they could just make out the shape of a horse, rising from the water.

The horse was unlike any horse they had ever seen before—or would ever be likely to see again. Twice as big as Lethavian's steed, and seemingly made of flesh, bone and liquid. As it reared up onto its back legs the four friends could see their reflections in its silvery, almost mirror-like, body.

"This, my friends, is a water horse. Another of my little creations and, I must say, one of my best yet," said Theodore.

"It's amazing! Truly amazing! I can't quite believe what I'm seeing." The two boys could only stare in wonder as Erin spoke.

"Believe it, child, believe it. Now hurry, we have no time at all to waste, climb on—she won't hurt you," said Theodore, no sign of his grin disappearing.

Erin climbed on first, with a little help from Cameron and Finn who quickly followed her. The horse was comfortable to sit on; it had a friendly face and a flowing mane of pure blue water.

"Look at this," said Cameron as he stroked the horse's liquid body.

"My hand is completely dry; the water's not wet. Amazing!"

Both boys lent down towards Theodore, grabbed his arms and helped him up.

"Right; are we all sitting securely? Now which way did you say Lethavian went?" asked Theodore.

Erin, Finn and Cameron pointed to where The Dark Spirit had disappeared from sight.

"Then hold on tightly," instructed Theodore as he began speaking to the horse; "my beautiful horse; my beautiful lady of the lake; deliverous, deliverous."

No sooner had the words been spoken than the water horse reared up onto its back legs, and began to move off, heading towards the centre of the lake. It glided, effortlessly, over the surface of the water in the direction of The Dark Spirit.

****

As Lethavian neared the water's edge, the sack, draped over his horse's back, began to wriggle uncontrollably. His prize, claimed in the forest was certainly still very much alive. The sack bounced around before slipping off the horse and plunging into the icy depths of the lake. Lethavian desperately tried to hold on to his spoils but the weight was too great and the sack was torn from his fingers. He was helpless to do anymore than watch it—and its contents—sink out of sight.

He showed no hesitation, but continued on his way.

The sack sank quickly as if filled with lead; only stopping once it reached the cold, rocky bed at the bottom of the lake. For a while it danced about, as if a wild beast were trapped inside. Whatever it contained, it was not ready to be parted from this life; not just then at least.

After a short—but energetic—struggle, the sack relinquished in defeat, burst open and spewed out its secret.

The figure of a man cut through the water; lungs bursting, desperate for breath. It shot to the surface and filled its body with oxygen.

Disorientated, Theodore forced himself through the water and dragged himself onto the shore.

Chapter 11

VANDOR

The Shellac warriors descended the outer walls of the moss caves with speed. Willie and Lackey were cocooned in the centre of the group and had no option but to keep up with the Shellac warriors in front of them.

"I hope ye ken where ye're taking us?" asked Willie of the Shellac—all of them.

His question was not answered, in fact it was totally ignored, without even an acknowledgement.

"I take it ye do then," said Willie, chuckling to himself, amused by the lack of communication.

"Don't worry, friend. The way is known," said Lackey, struggling to keep up.

It was only a short while before the group found themselves, once again, in the thick undergrowth of the Black Forest. The many stars in the sky soon disappeared from sight, eclipsed by the dense canopy of leaves towering above them.

The lead group of Shellac warriors suddenly came to an abrupt halt. A shadow—as large as the moon itself—passed over them. The shadow passed smoothly, if ominously, disappearing as quickly as it had appeared. The tops of the trees waved to and fro in the vortex created by whatever had just flown over them.

"What the heck was that?" asked Willie, stumbling over several Shellac warriors who had come to a halt directly in front of him.

Lackey gazed upwards, through the blanket of trees and into the sky, the fear in his eyes all too obvious.

"Nothing, friend. Nothing but angry clouds in sky," replied Lackey, hoping that Willie would neither see, nor sense, his fear.

The group soon continued, silently, on their way. Communication between the Shellac was limited; occasionally they would nod, or point to each other, but they never spoke. The Shellac had travelled through the Black Forest many times, usually on hunting trips. They had first hand knowledge of the dangers; that lurked in the forest. Having, lost, many of their fellow Shellac to The Dark Spirit, within its perimeters. It was that knowledge and experience that kept them going.

The forest path twisted and turned; the foliage and undergrowth was so dense it was almost claustrophobic. As the Shellac warriors were busy, using their axes to clear a way through the undergrowth, a Black Hammer caught the eye of one of the more observant amongst them.

The Black Hammer was perched high in a tree, watching them move across the forest floor below—its evil yellow eyes feeding information back to its master. The Black Hammer sat silently, head cocked to one side, as the same shadow that had previously passed over them appeared once more above them. It passed effortlessly overhead, throwing Willie, Lackey and the Shellac warriors into almost total darkness.

"What is...?"

Lackey quickly interrupted Willie before he had chance to finish his sentence. "Shhh! Willie must remain silent. *He* will hear us," he said, holding a finger against his lips.

The shadow hung above them for a moment before moving away and disappearing from sight.

The Black Hammer remained perched in its tree, its yellow eyes still fixed on the group below.

"Black Hammer betrays our location," said Lackey, pointing to the evil bird with his skinny finger.

One of the Shellac warriors grabbed his axe and threw it at the bird. The axe span, like a Catherine Wheel on bonfire night, at speed towards the Black Hammer. It sliced through the forest, severing vines and branches on its way; like a strimmer through grass.

The winged spy caught sight of the axe as it got nearer. The evil bird jumped from its perch to take flight, but it was too late. The axe severed the bird in two without loosing momentum and continued to spin through the air. It circled, like a boomerang, before heading back towards the group. Willie's eyes remained fixed on the axe, as it flew towards him.

"TAKE COVER!" shouted Willie, at the same time pushing Lackey into the undergrowth, before diving for cover himself.

The Shellac warrior who had thrown the axe stood firm, tracking its progress as it approached. He lifted his hand and caught the axe firmly by its handle, without flinching a single muscle. He then wiped the blade of the axe on his trouser leg before re-securing the axe to his belt.

Lackey rose from the undergrowth, unable to control his laughter. "Quickly, TAKE COVER," he repeated, mocking his giant of a friend.

Willie lifted himself from the forest floor. His face was covered in mud, with clumps of bog-weed protruding from his mass of orange hair.

Lackey continued to laugh and was even joined by the Shellac warriors, who found the whole situation quite amusing.

Willie stood, frowning at them all, but his frown soon turned into a beaming smile.

"What a man has tae do, to get some communication aroond here," said Willie, joining in with the laughter.

As the group continued through the forest the dense undergrowth gave way to more sparsely-covered ground, which aided their progress. They travelled at speed now, heading toward Lethavian's inner-evildom. The air temperature increased the further they travelled. Willie's throat becoming quite dry, he found it increasingly difficult to breathe, the air seemingly burning his lungs.

"Is it me, or has someone turned the heat up?" he asked, his huge frame simply awash with sweat, as he stumbled along.

"Yes friend, is getting hotter, we get nearer the lava fields," replied Lackey.

"What lava fields?" asked Willie, rolling his eyes into the back of his head in disbelief.

"Lava fields surrounding Dark Spirit's inner-evildom!" exclaimed Lackey, perspiration mounting on his brow.

"Lava temperature, over a gillion thermo bars," he continued.

Willie rolled his eyes into the back of his head again. "Yer not kidding, I feel like I'm melting."

As they continued, not only did the temperature in the forest increase, but so did the light, since the lava gave off an orange glow. It reminded Willie of a flaming sunrise, bursting across a dark Scottish sky. It warmed his spirit.

The forest began rapidly to disappear, giving way to a barren area of land where no vegetation could survive due to the lack of moisture. The group stopped on the very edge of the barren land, beneath what appeared to be the last remaining tree. Its mangled and twisted branches had been stripped of leaves, but it gave enough cover from any prying eyes above.

The lava fields were now visible to the group, being just ahead of their position. They resembled a series of small lakes, spread over a huge area, all glowing with the sticky orange lava that filled them. The sky was alight with the penetrating glow and the ground was lit for quite some distance in all directions.

One of the Shellac warriors removed several flasks of water, which he'd been carrying around his waist on a belt, and passed them around the group.

"Ahh, I needed that!" exclaimed Willie as he emptied the flask.

"From here we must move as quickly as we can. We must cross the lava fields, then head for the cover of the salt mines—the doorway to The Dark Spirit," said one of the Shellac warriors.

"Yes, Narabius. I will tell them," said the warrior, staring at Willie and Lackey. "You must wear your moss boots, they will give you protection from the heat of the lava."

"Narabius? We left him a long way back, in the moss caves," said Willie, looking puzzled.

"His body, yes; but his mind travels with us," replied the Shellac warrior.

Willie remained silent, choosing simply to accept the response. In fact he would probably have accepted anything that was suggested to him right now, being quite overwhelmed by the whole experience.

The group quickly pulled on their moss boots, before leaving the cover of the tree, and heading towards the lava fields.

The group moved quickly, not wanting to spend a moment longer than was absolutely necessary in the open. The Shellac warriors took up a diamond formation, surrounding Willie and Lackey, to give them maximum protection from all sides.

"Keep moving friend, not waste time in this place," said Lackey, urging Willie on.

Willie hesitated slightly as he reached the edge of the lava field. The Shellac warriors showed no sign of stopping—or even slowing down—which forced Willie onto the lava after them.

"Keep moving, friend. Keep moving," said Lackey, aware that potential danger lurked all around.

"I can't believe it, the moss boots are keeping ma feet cool, I can't even tell I'm walking on lava!" exclaimed Willie with a look of amazement across his face. The lava was the consistency of mud, allowing the group to walk on its surface. If they stood still for to long however it would suck them in.

"Believe, friend. Moisture trapped deep in moss will protect from intense heat, at least," Lackey paused momentarily, "at least five of your minutes."

"Five minutes ye say? Then what?" asked Willie.

Lackey began to chuckle before giving his response.

"Your feet will BOIL!"

Willie wiped the sweat from his forehead, the shock of Lackey's response striking him dumb; he lengthened his stride across the lava.

The salt mines were clearly visible to the group, and getting closer all the time, as they made their way across the orange-glowing lava fields. Willie began to relax a little as the edge of the lava got closer, and firmer ground came into sight. His relief was evident by the smile which slowly found its way back onto his face. The moss boots continued to fight off the heat of the lava, although with each step their feet became warmer.

Willie suddenly noticed a shadow passing over them, a large and imposing shadow, the same one which had already passed over them, twice, in the Black Forest.

Willie glanced upwards, his concentration on reaching the salt mines momentarily broken.

"WHAT IS THAT?" he screamed, unsure what was happening.

The Shellac warriors and Lackey lifted their eyes to the sky.

"VANDOR," screamed Lackey

"VAN-WHAT?" asked Willie.

"VANDOR,THE FIRE DRAGON!" exclaimed Lackey as the large dragon-like creature, now directly above them, began to spit red-hot fireballs the size of dinner plates towards them.

The Shellac warriors quickly tightened their formation around Willie and Lackey. They had been sent by Narabius, the wise elder of the Shellacs, to ensure safe passage, so that they might reach The Dark Spirit and destroy him; and that is exactly what they intended to do.

The warriors deflected the fireballs with their axes, their only weapon but one which they had all mastered. The force of the attack and the heat from the lava soon began to drain their energy.

"We must defend, but also keep moving. We have no time to stand still," advised the lead Shellac, as they carefully continued to edge their way towards the salt mines. They held their formation well, encircling Willie and Lackey, protecting them from the barrage of fireballs rained upon them by Vandor.

Vandor was a strange-looking creature, resembling a cross between the magical phoenix and a mythical dragon. His body was certainly dragon-like, but his huge wings, which allowed him to soar gracefully through the sky, were bird-like, each feather being the size of Willie. His eyes were yellow and evil-looking, just like the Black Hammers; his mouth, home to a terrifying collection of teeth. He had a long, pointed, face which, like his body, was covered in dark brown scales, resembling a piece of old leather. His legs and feet were bird-like, with powerful thighs and claws, which glistened like newly-sharpened knives.

Vandor had been created by The Dark Spirit, to protect the entrance to the salt mines, the doorway to his inner-evildom. The mere existence of Vandor left The Dark Spirit confident that his inner-fortress was impregnable.

The group continued to move towards the salt mines, whilst Vandor continued to attack. He soared high above them, circling, before diving at the group. Vandor swept over them, legs outstretched, claws poised. The Shellac warriors swung their axes at him, attempting to maim—or at least injure—the fearsome creature. The axes made contact, but Vandor was still able to bury his clawed feet into the warriors—his leathery skin was tough, and the axes made little impression.

Having left several Shellac warriors dead on the ground, Vandor singled out one in particular. He mercilessly sank his talons into the poor little creature, who screamed in agony, before taking once more to the sky. The Shellac hostage was now, no more than a rag doll to him. He perched himself on top of the salt mines, where he could be seen devouring his prey.

Vandor feasted quickly, taking only moments to consume the brave warrior. He wasted nothing, devouring armour, clothes, bones and all. Vandor then fixed his eyes on the remaining members of the group, who had now all but reached the salt mines. he dropped from his perch to unleash another attack.

Willie caught sight of Vandor as he dived towards them.

"HE'S COMING BACK, RUN FOR THE MINES," he shouted, warning the others of the impending danger. The formation of the group broke as they rushed for the salt mines in panic.

Willie noticed his feet starting to get hot as the last of the moisture, held deep within his moss boots, was dried up by the constant and intense heat of the lava.

"MA FEET, THEY'RE ON FIRE," he screamed as he grabbed Lackey by the scruff of the neck and dived off the lava field, onto firm ground at the foot of the salt mines. There he quickly tore off the moss boots, exposing his own, smouldering, boots underneath. He took his hunting knife from his back pack and severed his laces, kicking his boots off to cool his feet.

"ARGH, ma toes are scorching!"

The remaining Shellac warriors leapt onto the ground beside Willie and Lackey as Vandor struck again.

The Shellac warriors fended him off as best they could, waving axes, arms and legs in all directions, vainly attempting to protect themselves. Vandor's size and strength soon overpowered the remaining, exhausted Shellacs, and he sank his claws into them, grabbing hold of one poor soul before taking flight once more to feast.

The four remaining Shellac warriors stood in silence, along with Willie and Lackey, unable to do anything to save their friend. Uninterrupted Vandor consumed the warriors body, claiming his soul for his master—The Dark Spirit.

Willie bent down and picked up an axe from the ground. It had been dropped by one of the Shellac warriors claimed by Vandor. As he lifted the axe the jewels that encrusted its handle started to glow, sending a prism of light shooting up his arm. His vision became fixed on the light, which resembled a rainbow; it ran up his arm and over his shoulder. From there it stretched along the base of the salt mines and came to rest on a small opening.

"That's it, look! That's the way in," said Willie, pointing to the opening. He smiled to himself, aware that Narabius continued to guide them.

Willie's smile soon disappeared, however, as the prism of light faded away when Vandor's shadow raced across the ground towards them.

"Head for the entrance. We will fend him off," instructed one of the Shellac warriors.

Willie, Lackey and two of the warriors headed for the opening that had been revealed by the prism of light, while the other two warriors bravely remained to face Vandor. As they reached the entrance, Willie turned to where the Shellac had stood, but nothing remained. The warriors had gone; Vandor also.

Willie felt an uncontrollable wave of anger flooding through his body, anger for The Dark Spirit; for allowing such disregard for the lives of others to exist in this world.

Suddenly, a fireball struck the ground at Willie's feet; he looked up and saw Vandor, diving towards him at speed, ready to attack. Willie stood firm. He had seen enough blood shed on his behalf and would stand and fight, determined to destroy Vandor once and for all. He gripped the axe tightly in his hand, ready for battle.

"Friend, come quickly! Vandor close." Lackey's words drifted in—and then out—of Willie's head. He had made his decision and nothing would change his mind.

Another fireball struck the ground close to Willie as Vandor attacked. The huge Scot ducked and turned, Vandor's claws missing only narrowly. Willie swung the axe with all his might, its blade sank deep into Vandor's leg as he took flight back into the sky.

Willie had now been joined by Lackey and the remaining two Shellac warriors.

"Willie; friend; cannot fight Vandor. Must leave now he'll claim us all," said Lackey, taking hold of Willie's hand.

"Fight him? Why ma wee friend, I have no intention of fighting him—but I am going to destroy him." Willie smiled, before quickly removing his slingshot from his webbing belt. He then carefully removed a piece of old cloth from his back pack and unwrapped it to expose two small glass phials of Pixie Pogrom.

Lackey looked on inquisitively. "Lackey not understand. Will take more than ointment to destroy Vandor."

Willie's smile grew wider. "This is no ordinary ointment friend. *This* is Pixie Pogrom."

Lackey still did not understand, but kept a close watch as Willie handled one of the phials with great care, delicately placing it into his sling. A shadow quickly engulfed them as Vandor returned to the sky above. A fireball screeched towards Lackey, who dived for cover. It struck the ground just a short distance from Willie, breaking his concentration and causing him to fumble; the phial of Pixie Pogrom, which fell from his fingers and onto the ground at his feet.

The small glass phial did not break, but in a split second it had rolled away from Willie and into the molten lava of the lakes where it slowly sank from view.

Another fireball struck, close enough to Willie to knock him off his feet. Vandor attacked relentlessly, raining fireball after fireball down upon the group.

Vandor swooped down, claws exposed, ready to rip through flesh and bone. However, just as he prepared for the killer blow, the lava below him erupted, sending a red-hot molten column shooting skywards—like a volcano blowing its top. The lava hit Vandor in the stomach, sending him reeling upwards, away from the group. Lackey and the two remaining Shellac warriors gawped in amazement as Vandor was tossed into the sky.

"Narabius. He said he would guide us along," said one of the Shellac warriors, looking rather humble.

"Narabius ma hat!" exclaimed Willie. "That, ma friends, was the Pixie Pogrom. I wondered what would happen once the lava had melted through the glass phial." He smiled excitedly as he carefully took the remaining phial of Pixie Pogrom and placed it gently into his sling.

The sky above the group began to fill with thick, black, angry-looking clouds, and a strong wind started to blow.

"The Dark Spirit is angry. We must leave this place. Now!" insisted one of the Shellac warriors.

Willie stood his ground, "not until I rid the sky of that dragon," he said, pointing into the sky at Vandor who was rapidly approaching.

"COVER YOURSELVES!" shouted Willie as he shut one eye, focusing the other on Vandor. He steadied himself for a moment before releasing the sling. The small glass phial flew through the air like a bullet towards its target. Willie dived to the ground, covering his head with his hands as the Pixie Pogrom struck Vandor in the centre of his chest. The phial shattered into a thousand pieces; the liquid Pixie Pogrom contained within it also exploded, consuming everything it touched.

Lackey glanced into the sky as Vandor disappeared with a deafening boom and a flash of light—so bright, it seemed as though a thousand shooting stars were passing overhead. The bright light soon faded away, however, and was replaced with the orange glow from the lava. The angry-looking clouds were gone, as was Vandor. The strong wind had died down and a deathly silence fell all around.

The remaining Shellac warriors stood, gob-smacked; staring into the sky, not quite believing that Vandor had finally been defeated.

Willie stood proud; satisfied with the outcome; satisfied that they could now continue on their mission to destroy The Dark Spirit, his defences now even further weakened.

Lackey took Willie's hand as the group entered the salt mines.

Chapter 12

THE EYES OF THE BEHOLDER

The water horse was truly a lady of the lake. Her beauty and elegance mesmerised all who rode upon her, she glided effortlessly across the surface of the water.

The cooling breeze blew through Cameron's long orange hair; tears ran down his cheeks as his eyes watered uncontrollably.

"Wah hey! This is better than any fairground ride I've ever been on," he said, the experience almost taking his breath away.

"Me too," replied Finn, holding his arms outstretched at his side, allowing the cool air to rush through his fingers.

Erin remained silent, clinging desperately to her brother who sat directly in front of her. She was not one for white-knuckle rides, nor any fairground ride in fact, preferring to keep both feet firmly on the ground. She closed her eyes tightly, hoping that they would soon reach their destination.

Theodore sat, smugly, behind them all; a grin still etched upon his face. This was, without question, one of his better creations and one of which... he was extremely proud.

As the horse carried them across the lake they rapidly approached the opposite shoreline.

"Our journey will soon be over," said Cameron, rather disappointedly.

Before anyone had a chance to reply, and without warning, the sky lit up by a colossal flash of light. The light was quickly followed by a deafening boom, so loud it was as if the world itself had exploded. The boom spooked the water horse; so much so that once again it reared onto its back legs, this time tossing the four friends off its back and into the water. The horse then dived beneath the surface and disappeared from sight.

Finn was the first to emerge. He shot through the surface of the icy water, spluttering and gasping as he gulped his first breath. He was quickly followed by the other three, all of whom struggled to refill their lungs, as the icy water gripped and squeezed at their chests.

"Is....is...is everyone OK?" mumbled Cameron, the shock from the cold water making it difficult for him to speak.

"C....c...cold," replied Erin, having to force the word out.

Theodore and Finn were unable to speak, but nodded in turn.

Erin grabbed hold of Theodore as the four friends slowly started to make their way through the water, towards the shoreline.

A strange undercurrent slowed their progress. It was as if unseen hands had taken hold of their legs, weighing them down and sapping their strength. The four friends struggled to make their way through the water, the weight of their wet clothes weighing them down, as the souls of the departed, desperately, tried, to drag them under.

Finn, cold and exhausted, closed his eyes and slowly sank beneath the surface of the water. He had given up, his energy was gone. The freezing water had made his body so stiff, it was as though he was paralysed. Cameron saw what was happening to his friend. He quickly dived down through the water, just managing to grab Finn by the scruff of his neck before he disappeared completely from sight. He pulled with every ounce of energy left in his body, dragging Finn back to the surface of the lake.

"Theodore, you must do something, we cannot make it on our own," said Cameron, teeth chattering.

The undercurrent continued to slow them down; it felt as though they were dragging lead weights behind them.

Theodore coughed and spluttered as he cleared his throat. "Deliverous; deliverous," he chanted, in a faint but determined voice.

The water beneath them bubbled, sending pockets of air to the surface. The bubbling intensified—like a pan coming to the boil—until, suddenly, the water horse emerged from the water beneath them. The friends clambered onto its back and were quickly carried out of the icy water.

The horse glided across the water's surface. It came to a halt at the shoreline. Rearing once more onto its back legs, it tossed its passengers off its back and onto the pebbly ground where they lay cold and exhausted, but alive.

The water horse then turned and dived back into the lake, beneath the surface and out of sight.

Theodore was first to stir. Wearily he picked himself up, wringing the water from his cassock. "That was unexpected, a Water Horse spooked by a clap of thunder! Well I suppose it *was* quite loud. Must have used too much Scary Cat Root in the potion," he muttered to himself as the others began to stir.

"Is everyone OK?" asked Erin, as she stood up and emptied the water from her pockets.

"Fine," replied Cameron.

"OK," answered Finn, "just wet, cold and tired," he shivered as he spoke.

"Come along, dry yourselves and get warm by the fire," urged Theodore.

The three friends looked at each other in amazement.

"I think the cold is affecting his head," whispered Cameron.

"What fire?" asked Erin.

"Why this one. Just here," replied Theodore, smiling as he pointed to the ground just in front of himself.

"Thermalous." No sooner had the word left his mouth than the ground erupted into a blaze of flames. There, in front of them, was the most welcoming and warming campfire they had ever seen.

The four friends soon began to dry out and their body temperatures quickly returned to normal.

"What do you think the noise was that spooked the water horse, Theodore?" asked Erin.

"I am not sure, my child. An atmospheric phenomenon, perhaps," he replied, stroking his beard; unaware that it had, in fact, been Willie—destroying Vandor with the Pixie Pogrom.

Erin smiled. She did not know what Theodore was talking about, but it sounded convincing.

"Does anyone know where we are?" asked Cameron, glancing around.

They were sitting on the edge of the lake, in a very dry and barren area of land which spread out in front of them for as far as they could see.

"I haven't got a clue, but I guess we go that way," said Finn, pointing away from the lake to the distant horizon.

The four friends, now dry and rested, prepared themselves to continue in their search for The Dark Spirit. Finn stood up and kicked some dirt into the fire, dampening its flames.

"Right let's get going," he said, grabbing Theodore and pulling him to his feet.

Theodore was startled by being hauled up, in such a fashion.

"I see your energy and strength have returned," he said, brushing himself down.

"Sorry, Theodore. I just want to find him," replied Finn.

"And so you shall, so you shall," smirked Theodore, as they cautiously began to make their way after Lethavian.

****

Cameron's hunting skills (honed through endless days snaring rabbits and tracking wild boar with Willie around their home in the forest where they lived) soon became useful.

"Look, there. It's a hoof print, left by a horse; a large one at that. It must be Lethavian's black charger," he said, as he knelt on the ground and ran his finger around the curved mark that was imprinted into the dry, salty earth.

"There are two sets of prints," said Finn pointing to the ground. "But we saw only one horse." He knelt next to Cameron to study the ground in more detail.

"Definitely two sets," he said once more.

Cameron started to laugh, "you'd be no good hunting with me. I'd be dizzy going round in circles, chasing my tail."

"What do you mean?" asked Finn, screwing his face up in disgust.

Cameron continued to laugh. "Look! Look at the shape of the hooves; do you see?" he asked, pointing at the salty earth.

Finn stared hard, but could not understand what Cameron meant.

"One set of prints running toward the lake, the other set running away; see? One horse, two sets of prints—one outbound, the other from the return journey," said Cameron as he messed, jokingly, with Finn's hair.

Finn did not reply but turned red with embarrassment, at the same time grinning at his own mistake.

"Follow the prints, quickly! They will lead us to him," said Theodore, urging the group on.

****

A solitary Black Hammer struggled to fly through the cold black sky. It had a broken wing, sustained in the Black Forest, trying to claim the soul from a poor, unsuspecting, Shellac. Its beak was stained red with blood and its belly full. It had feasted on the tiny morsels left by Vandor and was now looking for a secluded perch on which to sit and digest its food. Its progress was slow, being weighed down by its own selfish greed. Although desperate to find shelter, the Black Hammer was too exhausted and in too much pain to fly any further and so it settled—exposed—on the dry, salty earth.

****

The four friends made good progress by letting the hoof prints guide them along. Ahead, just in the distance, they could make out the shape of the solitary, exhausted, Black Hammer. The bird sat quite still, without energy to do anything but move its head, listening to the sounds carried on the breeze.

"Theodore, just ahead of us is a Black Hammer. It's on the ground; it must have broken its wing. It's definitely not moving," said Erin.

The Black Hammer remained quite still. As the four friends cautiously approached, it cocked its head and spat, but was unable to do little more.

"Do not let it escape," ordered Theodore. "Capture it, I must have its eyes."

Cameron did not hesitate. He threw his webbing sack over the bird and trapped it on the ground.

"Got it!" he screamed excitedly as he lifted the bird into his arms. "Shall I kill it?" he asked.

Theodore nodded. "Make it quick and painless—and do not damage its eyes."

Cameron responded immediately. With the bird's neck between his fingers, he flicked his wrist. It was all over in less than a second and the lifeless body hung limply in his hand.

"CAMERON! HOW COULD YOU?" shouted Erin.

Cameron just smiled. "It didn't feel a thing, besides its wing was damaged, it would have died a slow, painful, death, if we had just left it." he said proudly.

"Do not upset yourself, Erin. The bird was pure evil, and now it is at peace; released from Lethavian's control." Theodore's words obviously reassured Erin as the colour soon started to return to her pale cheeks.

"What do you want its eyes for?" asked Finn, confused at Theodore's request.

"Why, to see again! To see Lethavian; to guide us to him," he replied, "dig me a hole Cameron—big enough to bury the Black Hammer."

Cameron did as Theodore asked, using his hands to dig through the crusty earth. Theodore carefully removed the eyes from the Black Hammer, applying pressure to the side of the bird's head to pop them out. He then carefully wrapped the eyes in a piece of cloth, before slipping them into a pocket beneath his cassock.

Cameron took the bird from Theodore and placed it into the hole, covering it over with the loose earth he had created through his efforts.

"Take my hand, child. Place it on the grave," said Theodore, kneeling down.

Erin did as she was asked.

Theodore muttered a few simple words before getting back to his feet.

"We must continue. Leave this place now, before we are spotted." Theodore took hold of Erin's arm and they continued; following the direction of the hoof prints, and getting closer to The Dark Spirit with every step.

After a long and gruelling trek across the arid, barren land, the four friends came across an opening in the ground. The hoof prints seemed to disappear into the opening.

Cameron, Erin, Finn and Theodore, now found themselves standing on top of the salt mines; unaware that they were not far from where Willie and Lackey had battled with Vandor.

"The horse must have entered here, I can see its prints running off down there," said Cameron, pointing down the mineshaft, which sloped away at a forty five degree angle.

"Then we must follow immediately," instructed Theodore, "my brother is waiting for us," he whispered to himself excitedly.

"Wait!" said Finn. "I can see something... over there!" He walked a few paces across to get a better look and found himself standing on the very edge of a cliff.

"This is like some kind of nest. Just look at the size of it!" his eyes widened as he looked around, unaware that he was standing in Vandor's home.

The nest was made out of large branches, lined with moss. It was perfectly round, and large enough to house an entire family of Shellac.

"WOW! Look at this!" shouted Finn as he struggled to lift a huge feather, easily as tall as he was.

Theodore, Erin and Cameron joined Finn, all mesmerised by the find.

"We cannot stay here, it is too dangerous," said Theodore, after Erin had explained where they were standing.

"For, if the owner of the feather returns, I fear that we will be very much on the menu."

Cameron stood silently, staring over the edge of the cliff, in total awe of the view which lay before him.

"Look at this! It's just unbelievable," he said, pointing below.

The lava fields dominated the ground at the immediate foot of the cliffs; beyond that, the Black Forest spread out into the distance. Erin explained to Theodore what lay ahead of them.

"Then we are here. Soon we shall all meet with him; these salt mines are the gateway to his inner-evildom."

A shiver ran down Erin's spine; Theodore's words brought home the reality of how close they were to The Dark Spirit.

"How do you know that *this* is the place? How do you know that *this* is the gateway to his inner-evildom?" asked Finn, keen to discover Theodore's source of information.

"He told me. Lethavian told me in the forest; when we were alone he told me I would find him—he told me many things." Theodore's face showed no emotion as he spoke.

Finn noticed the look of emptiness on Theodore's face, but said nothing.

Cameron stood on the edge of the cliff top, the lava fields held his concentration and he watched them bubbling and spitting below. The orange glow from the molten lava produced a warming band of light, which seeped into the cold dark sky. The cliffs were at least a hundred feet high and white, an effect of the salt which ran through the mines.

"I have never seen anywhere quite like this before; it is a truly amazing sight," said Cameron, as he turned to the others who had already left the nest and begun to make their way back to the entrance of the mines. As he turned, he caught his foot on something in the nest which sent him sprawling, onto his stomach.

'Ouch, what was that?' he asked himself, getting back to his feet. The floor of the nest was lined with feathers, leaves and other pieces of undergrowth, all of which had acted like a mattress to Vandor.

Cameron bent down and took hold of whatever he had just stumbled over. With a heave he lifted an axe from the floor of the nest; until then it had been camouflaged with leaves and other foliage. He lifted the axe up for a closer look. It was a beautifully crafted weapon with a jewel-encrusted handle. The axe had belonged to one of the Shellac warriors, vanquished by Vandor.

"Hey, look what I've found," he shouted to the others as he ran to catch up with them.

"What is it?" asked Erin, curious to see what Cameron was carrying.

"An axe—but look at the handle, it's covered in gemstones. This isn't just any axe; it can't be," replied Cameron, holding the axe tightly, proud of his find.

"You are right, Cameron. From the description you give, it sounds as though... you are holding one of only twelve axes of its kind, crafted by the finest Shellac silversmith to have ever graced this land. You will not find better quality anywhere else, in this world or your own.

"But what do you think it was doing in the nest?" asked Finn.

"A simple question to answer; Willie and Lackey. I see no other explanation," replied Theodore.

"My father—he has been here?" asked Cameron, the words racing from his lips.

"These special axes were given to the twelve finest, most courageous Shellac warriors by Narabius himself. He hand-picked them; they answer to no one but Narabius, wisest of all Shellac elders. I can only presume that the twelve Shellac warriors were sent by Narabius, to ensure Willie and Lackey safe passage in their quest which like ours, is to destroy The Dark Spirit."

"So he *has* been here?" asked Cameron once more.

"But the Shellac warrior who owned that axe is nowhere to be seen. They must have failed in their quest." Cameron's heart sank at the thought of his father coming to harm.

"Do not upset yourself, Cameron. As I said, *twelve* axes exist. You have one, therefore eleven remain—I would say those odds are more than promising." Theodore placed his hand on Cameron's shoulder.

"Shall we continue? If Willie and Lackey are here, then I am sure they would welcome our assistance."

Cameron smiled, "you're right, Theodore. We must continue—our quest is far from over." He squeezed the axe tightly in his hands as he spoke, determined to find Willie, Lackey—and Lethavian.

Finn looked at Theodore suspiciously. "How does he know all this?" he whispered to Cameron, who shrugged off the comment as if it was unimportant.

****

Theodore removed the small piece of cloth from the pocket in his cassock and carefully unwrapped it, exposing the eyes that he had previously removed from the Black Hammer.

"What are you doing with those disgusting things?" asked Erin, her nose curling up in dismay.

"You will see, my child; and, for the first time in quite a while, so shall I," replied Theodore.

Erin turned her head; not able to watch as Theodore carefully removed his own eyes, replacing them with those of the Black Hammer. He blinked hard—several times—before snapping his eyelids wide open to reveal his new, evil-looking, organs of sight.

"Oh, Theodore; that is disgusting; you look awful. I much prefer the old you," said Erin, reviling Theodore's new look.

Theodore did not answer but gave a wry, self-righteous, smile.

"So? Can you see?" asked Cameron.

Theodore nodded. "Yes, child. I *can* see. I can see *everything* now; quite clearly." Theodore began to laugh loudly, a strange and menacing laugh, one the children had not heard from him before.

"I have a whole new outlook on life now that I can see again. Come, we must get going. Hurry! I am sure Lethavian is close, we must find him before all is lost."

Theodore urged his three friends into the opening at the top of the salt mines. From there they descended into Lethavian's inner-evildom.

Theodore brought up the rear of the group. He continued to smile to himself as Lethavian's words flushed through his mind.

'Good brother. I am watching—bring me those children; unite with me.'

Lethavian now also tracked their progress, guided by Theodore's newly-restored vision.

"I will be with you soon, brother," whispered Theodore to himself as he motioned the group on.

Chapter 13

◇◇

PIEGUS

"Prepare my armies, prepare them for battle. I am almost ready. No one will stand in my way. I will extinguish the sun, banish the moon and crush life itself. The only colour to remain in this world shall be the warm, exhilarating, colour of black; nothing else shall exist." Lethavian's voice thundered from his lips as he gave instruction to Piegus.

Piegus had been claimed by Lethavian many moons ago, whilst still only a young Shellac. He was spared from death for the sole purpose of serving Lethavian. He lived in constant fear, but had become accustomed and compliant to Lethavian's demands.

"Yes master, as you will. The armies will be ready," replied Piegus, before scurrying off, and out of sight.

Lethavian sat back down into his chair, "intra vires, intra vires," he muttered to himself, before releasing a hideous laugh—so loud, it echoed in each corner of his evildom.

****

"Keep moving, we have no time to stand still. He is waiting for us," said Theodore, again urging the others on. His mind was racing, almost out of control.

"How do you know that he is waiting for us? Can you see him?" asked Erin, unnerved by Theodore's abrupt and newly-acquired manner.

"Yes child, I see everything; everything is quite clear—as it will be to you, very soon." Theodore grinned painfully, his evil-looking yellow eyes bulged with pleasure.

"Theodore, you're frightening me—you're not yourself. I'm sure those eyes are possessed," pleaded Erin with genuine concern.

"Don't worry child, you have nothing to fear. Soon it will all be over, and er..., just beginning!" exclaimed Theodore, but his words only confused Erin even more.

Before she had time to reply, Lethavian's menacing laugh reached them. It echoed along the passageway in which they were now walking. The menacing laugh made them shudder—like fingernails being scrapped along a chalkboard—Then silence.

"What was that?" asked Finn, the hairs on the back of his neck standing on end.

"Not sure—but not nice," replied Cameron, the colour draining from his, usually rosy, cheeks.

Theodore began to chuckle to himself, "that, my friends, is the sole purpose of our journey—I would recognise my brothers laugh anywhere."

"What? That was The Dark Spirit?" replied Cameron, his heart racing.

"Yes, child. Lethavian is now much closer than you think," said Theodore, continuing to chuckle to himself.

Cameron stared at Theodore, focusing on his evil yellow eyes; unsure what was really happening, but with an overbearing sense that everything was going terribly wrong. Theodore's glazed expression remained fixed. He appeared to be oblivious to the fact that Cameron was eyeballing him.

"Something isn't right," whispered Cameron to Finn, "just look at him, standing there, completely emotionless. He's not himself—and those eyes aren't helping things either."

Finn nodded, agreeing with his friend. "I suspected something, earlier. We must keep a close eye on him—he *definitely* isn't himself," he replied.

The four friends continued along the passageway, fully aware that they would soon *(very soon at that)* be coming face to face with The Dark Spirit himself.

The passageway was dimly lit. It was a strange sort of glow, one which appeared to be coming from within the white, salt-laden walls. It provided just enough light for each of the group to follow the person in front without falling over them. Theodore led the group, his newly restored vision meant he could do so. The others followed in single file, they found the going easier as their eyes slowly adjusted to their surroundings.

Erin, who was at the rear of the group, suddenly came to a halt.

She pivoted around to look back up the passageway, concentrating hard, aware that someone—or something—was watching her. It was similar to the feeling she had experienced many times before, except this time it was much more intense. She felt a bead of perspiration gathering on her top lip as, once more, she sensed a thousand eyes staring at her. She quickly turned back to the group and hurried to catch them up.

"Wait for me," she shouted nervously, fearing for her own safety. "Something is following us, I know it is—I can sense it." her voice trembled. She was so afraid that she ran straight into the back of Cameron, she was so desperate not to be left behind.

"It's alright, nothing will harm you, I promise," said Cameron reassuringly as he removed his catapult and a few stones from his rucksack. "You stay upfront with Theodore, I'll bring up the rear. I'm sure it will be something and nothing, you'll see."

Cameron wanted to believe his own words, but secretly he felt more scared than he had ever done before.

"You keep an eye on Erin and Theodore, and I'll bring up the rear," he instructed Finn.

As they slowly made progress, the light in the passageway faded away, leaving the group in almost total darkness.

"Are you OK?" asked Cameron; more for his own reassurance than anything else.

"Yes, we're OK... and still here—but I can't see a thing," came Finn's reply.

The hairs on the back of Cameron's neck stood on end. Someone or—more to the point something—was behind him. He turned about, lifted and loaded his catapult in one swift movement. Staring into the darkness, Cameron gripped the handle as if his life depended on it.

"Who's there?" he demanded in a firm, but not over-confident, voice. He waited for what seemed like forever for a response; it did not come.

"Who's there? Speak now—or suffer the consequences," he demanded once more, his whole body shaking uncontrollably.

Cameron stood, fixed to the spot. The only sound he could hear was that of his heart beating—like a drum—deep within his chest. His throat tightened, his body tensed in anticipation. His breathing became shallow; the palms of his hands, sticky with sweat. The fear for his own safety was well founded. He now sensed something just ahead. With no time to think, he released the stone from his catapult—praying that it would find its target. He listened attentively as the stone flew through the air with speed. Cameron feared the sound of his heart, pounding, would drown out any other noise. Then the stone made contact with something. A strange noise met Cameron's ears—almost like a Wellington boot, squelching through mud. He smiled, happy in the knowledge that the stone had indeed made contact with its target.

His smile soon disappeared when he heard the stone once more, striking the wall of the passageway and falling to the ground. Desperately he fumbled in the dark in an attempt to reload his catapult. The cold, slimy, hands of a Mudthog slipped around his neck. His body went limp as he was lifted off the ground. The hands, now firmly around his neck, were squeezing the life out of him. The last thing he heard was a whooshing sound—like the blades of a helicopter slicing through the air—as his body dropped to the ground. Then came silence. Black; empty; silence.

"Cameron! Cameron laddie, wake up." the muffled sound of Willie's voice, slowly percolated through Cameron's unconscious mind. He could feel a hand on his shoulder, shaking him firmly.

"Cameron, you're safe now son; I'm here."

Willie's voice slowly became clearer as Cameron started to come round.

"Father—is that you?" he said as he opened his heavy eyes, focusing on the face of the man now kneeling in front of him.

The passageway was lit by a small lantern—carried by Thorner, one of the two remaining Shellac warriors. Cameron felt relief surging through his body as Willie's features became clearer.

"Yes laddie—it's me! You're safe now," replied Willie.

Cameron glanced around. Standing beside Willie was Lackey, close behind them stood Thorner and Hatcher, the two Shellac warriors. Thorner held the lantern, while Hatcher gripped tightly to his jewel encrusted axe. It had been that axe making the noise like a helicopter—whooshing through the air before severing the head from the torso of the Mudthog and rendering it to dust at Cameron's side.

Cameron jumped to his feet, flinging his arms around his father as tears welled in his eyes. "Am I pleased to see you! I thought I was a goner." A broad smile spread across his face as he let out a huge sigh of relief.

"Where are Finn and Erin?" asked Willie, concerned for the welfare of his friends.

"Just ahead—look, with Theodore," said Cameron as he turned to point down the passageway which disappeared into darkness. The smile on his face turned sour when he realised his friends were gone.

"Father, they were just ahead... with Theodore," his eyes dropped and his heart sank as he spoke. "Father, I don't think Theodore is who we believed him to be. He, has become quite strange—distant and detached—ever since his meeting with The Dark Spirit, back in the Black Forest." Cameron's concern for Finn and Erin mounted. "We must follow, father—for I fear their very lives are at risk!"

****

The cold dark passageway housed many nooks and crannies, small pockets and hiding places. Piegus watched, listening to Willie and Cameron from one such hiding place. His ears like radar, gathering every possible scrap of intelligence.

Piegus had once been a happy and respected Shellac, a little strange perhaps, but liked by most. He had spent the early part of his life in the moss caves. He had been claimed by Lethavian whilst playing with friends in the Black Forest, many moons ago. His friends had all been killed, their spirits claimed. It is said that when Lethavian was at the point of claiming Piegus, he saw something deep in his soul; something evil; something black; something that excited him. Piegus was spared by Lethavian because of this, to serve and obey him alone—The Dark Spirit.

Piegus watched, listening to Cameron, Willie, Lackey and the Shellac warriors, until they set off, making their way after Finn, Erin and Theodore. Piegus then slipped back into the shadows, to alert his master's armies of the impending battle.

****

"Cameron? Cameron? Are you still there? Say something," asked Finn, staring hard into the thick blanket of darkness hanging in the passageway.

"Theodore, wait! Cameron has gone. He must have dropped behind. We can't see, or hear, him." Erin's voice trembled with concern for her friend.

"Wait!" exclaimed Theodore. "Out of the question! We have no time to waste. Lethavian has been patient, we cannot delay any longer."

"What? Theodore, just listen to yourself! We're talking about Cameron; *our friend* Cameron?—without whom we would probably all be dead by now! We must wait for him," replied Finn in disbelief.

"Er..., yes my child. Of course, you are right. What am I thinking? We shall stop and rest until Cameron catches up—I am sure he will not be long." Theodore stroked his beard as he spoke, his mind flitting between what was happening now, and what he knew would be happening soon.

The three friends waited patiently for Cameron. He soon caught up with them.

"At last! What happened to you?" asked Finn. "We were starting to worry."

"Nothing to worry about—just lost my way in the dark. Come on, let's keep going," replied Cameron, casting Theodore a sly glance as the four set off again, to search for The Dark Spirit.

****

Piegus had reached the throbbing heart of Lethavian's inner-evidom, deep within the salt mines. Cautiously he entered, peering over the walkway on which he now stood, observing the hive of activity below.

Mudthogs! hundreds of Mudthogs were being created to serve Lethavian. At the hub of all the activity was a boiling, bubbling, pool of mud—just like the one in the firing gallery. The only difference was that this mud pool was on a much larger scale—stretching to the most vile corners of hell. The evil there was so intense, it is said that Satan himself dared not enter. From within the molten pool emerged Mudthog after Mudthog. As if on a conveyor belt, they were formed, moulded and born at this very spot; all identical and all for the same purpose—to destroy anything (and everything) that stood in Lethavian's path.

A furnace stood close by, glowing red-hot from the fire burning within it. Twelve Mudthogs worked busily around the furnace; crafting, hammering and creating the most lethal-looking swords. The same black swords used by the Mudthogs to attack Finn, Cameron, Erin and Theodore.

Piegus's eyes sparkled, the very sight of all this activity excited him, and fed his evil streak—his mouth almost drooled. He removed a small horn from around his waist, puckered his lips and blew. it was a solitary, doleful note; it hanged in the air, catching... the attention of each and everyone of the Mudthogs below.

"The time has come my friends; our master requires our services," grinning as he spoke, Piegus summoned the Mudthogs to prepare themselves for whatever lay ahead.

****

The Shellac warriors cocooned Willie, Lackey and Cameron as they cautiously descended along the, now quite dark, passageway. The Shellac had excellent eyesight; it allowed them to see through the blanket of darkness—like stars penetrating a black sky. They constantly scanned for Mudthogs; aware that potential danger lurked around every corner, the closer they got to Lethavian's lair.

"I do hope Finn and Erin are OK! Theodore certainly wasn't himself," said Cameron, hoping that he would soon catch up with his friends.

"Don't worry laddie—I'm sure they will be fine. Theodore's just having an off day perhaps?" replied Willie reassuringly.

Cameron wanted to believe his father, but something at the back of his mind made him doubt his words.

"Theodore is friend of Shellac—trusted friend. He will not harm Finn, or Erin, Theodore is good," said Lackey upon seeing the anguish in Cameron's face.

"I know—I know. It's just me; worrying for worry's sake," replied Cameron, unaware he was being watched once more by Piegus who was on his return journey to his master, having alerted the army.

Piegus stood silently, squashed into a small crevice, again watching and listening as they passed him by. He smirked to himself; the thought of this small group pitting their wits against the might of his master amused him. Unable to hold it in, he let out a slight snigger which was instantly detected by Hatcher, at the rear of the group. The warrior span around, staring into the darkness of the passageway. He approached the crevice in which Piegus was hiding as the remainder of the group turned to see what was happening. Thorner lifted his lantern, to give as much light as possible. Piegus felt a bead of sweat trickling down his back as Hatcher leaned into the crevice, pushing his face into his.

Piegus shrieked with fright, pushed past the Shellac warrior and into the passageway. He began to run as fast as his legs would allow him, in an attempt to escape the group.

In the blink of an eye, Hatcher removed his axe from around his waist and sent it spinning towards Piegus—who had now almost disappeared back into the blanket of darkness. The axe cut through the air at lightening speed and, like a bee to a honey pot, connected with its target with pinpoint accuracy. The blade of the axe made no contact with Piegus but its handle smashed into his legs, knocking him off balance and reducing him to a tangled pile of arms and legs on the ground. The axe then circled around, finding it path safely back into the hands of its owner.

Willie, Lackey, Cameron and the Shellac warriors soon reached Piegus where he lay, dazed and confused, on the ground.

"Don't hurt me. Piegus friend. meant no harm," he pleaded, cowering behind his hands like a frightened child.

"Why did ye run from us if ye're friend and nae foe?" boomed Willie, hoping that a bit of intimidation would force the truth from the frail, pathetic creature laid before him.

"Piegus! So *this* is where you ended!" exclaimed Lackey as he poked his head around Willie's large frame.

"You know him Lackey?" asked Cameron.

"Oh yes. Lackey knows Piegus. we were friends, long ago—until..." Lackey paused momentarily, "Piegus claimed by Dark Spirit." Cameron's jaw dropped, surprised by Lackey's words.

"Then he cannot be trusted—nor allowed to escape," said Willie, grabbing Piegus by the arm.

Hatcher removed a length of rope from around his waist and bound Piegus's hands and legs together.

"Leave me alone. Master will protect me. You will only anger him further. The Dark Spirit is all-seeing." Piegus's eyes filled with evil as he spoke, but his protest was in vain as Hatcher threw him, effortlessly over his shoulder.

"We must continue. We have little time to waste," barked Thorner as the group set off once more, along the passageway.

Piegus continued to protest. "My master will destroy you—all of you. His armies prepare themselves to advance on your world. Soon nothing will remain. He will conquer all." Piegus drew his wrinkled face into a grin, "let me go and I will spare you join with us—just as Theodore has."

Piegus sniggered to himself, a deathly silence now hanging in the air.

"It is true! Theodore unites with his brother. You will not survive unless you join with them," he continued.

"Enough, put a sock in it wee man," said Willie, ramming a piece of cloth into Piegus's mouth. "We have come here for one purpose—and *nothing* will deter us from that."

The group—now even more determined—quickened their step; their fear for the safety of Erin and Finn was now greater than ever.

Piegus continued to protest, but with his voice muffled by the piece of cloth, he soon gave up and fell silent.

Chapter 14

THE SHELLAC ARMY

Several moons had now passed since Willie and Lackey had left the moss caves, guided by the twelve brave Shellac warriors. Unbeknown to them, their journey was being monitored and assisted by Narabius, wise elder of the Shellac kingdom. Indeed, his ability to speak directly into the minds of his warriors was responsible for leading them safely to Vandor—and beyond.

Narabius's wisdom was born of his extensive life experience. It had earn him the title of 'wise elder' and meant that he was treated with utmost respect by all Shellac. He had made many mistakes throughout his life; some foolish, some costly, but all invaluable. Narabius managed to turn each—and every—mistake to his advantage. He was a Shellac with a heart and a conscience. It was his conscience that compelled him to offer further assistance in the finding and destruction of The Dark Spirit. But now he felt responsible for the deaths of ten of the twelve Shellac that he'd sent to ensure safe passage to Willie and Lackey. He also felt an even greater responsibility; for the future of his kingdom as well as that of the entire Shellac community.

"Friends! *Dear* friends.... Several moons ago, two brave individuals left these very moss caves, guided by twelve of our finest warriors. They left on a mission which would change the lives of each and every one of us—more than that, the lives of *all* future Shellac generations."

Narabius stood on high, on a small platform which jutted out from a wall in the moss cave. He spoke in a calm, but determined, manner as he addressed the entire Shellac community.

"Their mission—to locate and destroy The Dark Spirit and to claim back the Purple Crystal, so it can be used to protect all of us from evil."

Narabius felt his throat tightening as he spoke, knotting with emotion and the desire to succeed.

"The Dark Spirit has pillaged our lands for long enough; taking our loved ones, destroying entire families. Very soon, if he is not stopped, he will destroy us all....... I stand before you today with a heavy heart, but with a clear head. I ask every one of you with an ounce of energy in your body to join with me, to help our friends complete their mission."

Narabius looked down upon the marketplace below. He looked into the eyes of the Shellac people staring back at him. He knew he was asking a lot, but he could not think of any other way.

"To those of you who are able—and willing—to help safeguard our future; I leave from the Golden Gates in exactly one moon phase."

Silence engulfed the whole of the Shellac nation as the reality (and enormity) of Narabius's request sank in.

The silence was quickly replaced with gasps of shock. Then, slowly at first, but with increasing speed—like matches striking their box—small pockets of conversation sparked up everywhere.

"Mad! He's mad. destroy The Dark Spirit indeed!"

"Safeguard our future? That's his job!"

"He's right, we can't just sit back and do nothing!"

The conversation spread like wildfire, until the entire Shellac marketplace hummed—like a generator pulsing with energy—as Narabius's request was debated.

"Well done, Narabius. You're not such an old fool after all," said Coralada, placing her arm around him as they descended back into the heart of the Shellac kingdom.

"This might be our last chance. For as long as I can remember, I have waited for exactly this moment. Perhaps it should have come sooner..." Narabius spoke with concern, praying that his decision had not been made to late.

"Foolish decisions are made in haste. Wise decisions, on the other hand, are taken at a slower pace," replied Coralada, smiling reassuringly.

The activity in the marketplace had now reached fever pitch. Moss boots; swords; axes—and a whole range of armour, tin helmets, chain mail body suits, leg and thigh protectors, gloves, even gum shields were snapped up by would-be Shellac warriors. Most market traders gave freely, but a few (not so scrupulous) of them, used the opportunity to swell their coffers with gold.

Coralada escorted Narabius to her home.

"I'll put the stove on, a nice cup of nettle tea is just what we need," she said as Narabius took a seat at a small table.

From under his arm he removed a long, thin, wooden box, which he carefully placed on the table. He unhooked the three gold clasps which kept the box sealed, before nervously lifting the lid to expose its contents. A smile spread across his face, his eyes sparkled like diamonds. All was in place—nothing broken, or missing. Delicately, he scooped the contents from the box, lifting them up like a new-born baby being presented to the world for the first time. Narabius was holding the most beautifully-crafted bow ever to have been made. The bow—believed to have been carved by the gods themselves—was fashioned from a single piece of willow. It was elegantly-shaped, and strung with a single strand of angel hair. Housed beside the bow, in the box, were six silver-tipped arrows; so sharp, they could penetrate a solid stone wall and still find their target a mile away.

"Here you are, Narabius. Drink up!" said Coralada, placing a steaming-hot mug of nettle tea in front of him.

Narabius sat silently, sipping at his tea and pondering the events that lay ahead.

****

The sound of a solitary horn being blown broke the early-morning silence. It hung in the air, calling the Shellac kingdom to life with its dulcet tone.

Narabius awoke and lifted his head from the table, on which he had fallen asleep the night before. A blanket, placed over him by Coralada, slipped from his shoulders to the floor, exposing the bow which he still gripped firmly in his hand.

"The time has come! I shall not return until The Dark Spirit is no more," he whispered to himself, as he stood to his feet and removed the six, silver-tipped arrows from their housing. Gently, he placed the arrows into a leather quiver, which he then tied to his belt.

"Godspeed, Narabius. Bring yourself—and Lackey—home safely," said Coralada, bidding him farewell.

Narabius smiled back at her, before turning and leaving her home. As he walked into the Shellac marketplace, the sight that greeted him was overwhelming. Hundreds of Shellac were making their way to the Golden Gates. Like ants working for the common good, they weaved in and out of the market stalls. Each new arrival served to swell the already-large gathering of Shellac still further.

The mood was tense as the crowd, awaited Narabius's commands.

Narabius descended the walkway from Coralada's home, his heart bursting with pride. As he got closer to the Golden Gates, silence again fell over the masses of Shellac. Hundreds of Shellac lined the way, prepared and ready! Each one willing to battle with the most powerful and evil being known to them; prepared to lay down their life, for the greater good of the Shellac race.

Narabius felt quite humble as he walked amongst them. The realisation of the gravity of the situation was etched upon each and every face.

Narabius had always tried to lead by example—and this occasion would be no different. He would lead from the front and was prepared to be the first to die.

As he reached the Golden Gates, he turned to address the crowd once more. The sight was overwhelming. He looked into the marketplace, then up into the dwelling areas, high in the walls of the moss caves. He could see, not hundreds, but thousands of Shellac. Young and old alike; every single Shellac in the community had turned out in support, either to fight with Narabius, or to bid their loved ones and friends farewell and a safe return.

"Friends; I stand before you a humble Shellac, for whom words cannot even begin to do justice. Our quest will be arduous and dangerous. Many of us—maybe all—will not return. If we are successful in our mission, those of us that do, will return to a better, safer place; not only for us, but for every generation to come—on that I give you my word." Narabius paused as a deafening cheer filled the moss caves.

"Our journey will take us through the Black Forest to the lava fields, from there we shall enter the inner-evildom of The Dark Spirit. Be strong of heart and clear of head, and we shall succeed."

Narabius's words were once again greeted with a deafening cheer which filled the moss cave like the roar of thunder.

"Godspeed to us all," he said as he turned to the gates. Two Shellac warriors heaved the gates open, allowing the Shellac army, led by Narabius, to march out. They marched through the twisting caves, over walkways and through narrow passageways, until they reached the mouth of the caves, and the edge of the Black Forest.

Narabius paused to observe the open ground that bordered the Black Forest, aware that the dangers which lay ahead were as real as the nervous feeling in the pit of his stomach. He remained focussed; cleared his head and concentrated purely only on the task in hand. He used his telepathic powers to communicate with every single Shellac in his army, telling them to remain calm, not to be overzealous and, at the same time, warning them of the many hidden dangers which lay ahead.

****

Thousands of Black Hammers had gathered in the sky, above the Black Forest. They swarmed together like bees, before drifting slowly, like an angry storm cloud, towards the moss caves.

****

Narabius led his army, across the area of open land and into the shadows of the Black Forest. They moved silently and with speed, oblivious to the Black Hammers which now hovered above them, hidden from sight by the dense blanket of trees.

Narabius noticed a change in the shadows as they began to flicker and dance around him, he then heard the muffled sound of wings beating the air furiously. He looked up into the canopy of leaves where he caught sight of a single, yellow, eye staring back at him.

"PREPARE YOURSELVES!" he shouted, at the top of his voice, as the swarm of Black Hammers crashed through the trees towards them. The evil birds took many of the Shellac by surprise, emerging through the trees as if from nowhere. The birds sank their razor-sharp beaks and talons into anything they could, ripping into flesh and bone. The Shellac responded immediately—franticly waving swords and axes in the air, severing heads, feet and wings from the birds. The wounded Black Hammers dropped at Shellac's, feet, but as one bird's life was extinguished, another took its place. Tens of thousands of birds attacked relentlessly, driven by Lethavian's greed and desire for violence.

The noise made by the birds was deafening; wings flapping, hearts beating—and the screeching... They descended like locus intent on destroying a corn field.

Disorientated by the mass of birds, yet still determined, the Shellac battled on; Narabius filled their minds with the strength to continue. Many of the Shellac were permanently scarred by the razor-sharp claws, some lost eyes and ears, some lost their lives—their very throats ripped out. The Shellac battled on bravely, encouraged by the news that the Black Hammers' attack appeared to be abating. Thousands of dead birds covered the forest floor, like a newly-laid—but blood streaked—carpet.

Exhaustion was becoming a very real threat, as were the Shadow Demons—which took advantage of any weakened Shellac's mind. The demons danced in and out of trees, twisting and changing shape as they went. They preyed on the weak and vulnerable; pinning them to the ground; starving them of energy as they squeezed the oxygen from their bodies. The Shadow Demons worked in groups, attacking the Shellac one by one, feeding on the misery caused by the slow, painful, death they inflicted on their prey. Desperately, the Shellac tried to fend off the demons with their weapons; swords and axes cut into the dark sky. Their efforts were all futile—their weapons had no effect—how could they against an evil that exists only in one's mind?

Narabius, unaware that many of his weakened troops were being lost to Shadow Demons, continued to battle with the Black Hammers. His body was wounded, but his mind remained strong and unblemished. The remaining birds reformed and took flight, back to Lethavian, nursing their wounds as they went.

Narabius sighed with relief, glancing around to survey the damage. Thousands of Black Hammers lined the forest floor—as did many of his Shellac warriors. Here and there, bands of Shellac still battled with the Shadow Demons, writhing in agony, as they sliced and stabbed their weapons into the air. Narabius now knew what was happening; he'd had first-hand experience of the Shadow Demons of the Black Forest, in his younger (and more naïve) days. He quickly removed a handful of silver fern from his pocket. He also removed a small bottle—filled with the water of life, which he sprinkled over the fern before squashing it into a tight ball in his hands. He attached the ball to one of his remaining, silver-tipped, arrows. The willow bow felt like silk in his hands. He gently pulled back on the angel hair, before releasing it from his fingertips. The arrow shot through the blanket of trees, high into the dark sky. It flew with speed, looking as if it would reach the moon itself, before bursting into flames and lighting the surrounding sky like a flare over a marooned ship. Narabius smiled as the light from the arrow filtered through the leaves, branches, and gaps in the tree-lined ceiling, to light up the forest floor. The light hung in the air, like clouds on a mountain top, restoring the ability to see to the Shellac and banishing the Shadow Demons back to their darkened corners.

"Gather our fallen brothers; lay them together—so we may collect them upon our return," instructed Narabius. "Any Shellac who has given their life for the better of our community shall be buried a hero."

The Shellac quickly did as Narabius asked. Those amongst them who were wounded, or could go no further, were given supplies of food and drink. They were instructed to wait for the returning party and to watch over the dead. Those Shellac prepared to continue looked once more to Narabius for guidance.

"We shall rest here tonight; take nourishment and sleep. We then head for the lava fields. Be proud of your achievements, but remember; victory today may be ours, but the real battle is just beginning." said Narabius, knelt, his head bowed in respect of his fallen friends as he addressed his army, through, telepathy.

The night was long. The Shellac took turns through the night to watch over their comrades.

The Shadow Demons showed no sign of returning, although most of the Shellac slept with their weapons held tight for fear of reprisals.

The following morning, Narabius's army was woken by a solitary bugler; his annoyingly cheery tune announced it was time to continue!

****

At the edge of the Black Forest they reached another stretch of open land, this time separating them from the lava fields. The sky glowed orange as the light from the molten lava oozed into the dark sky.

"What now?" asked one of the Shellac.

Narabius looked thoughtful as he stared at the lava fields.

"We must cross the lava, reach the cliffs beyond. That is where we shall find *him*."

The hum of conversation between the Shellac ceased, all now staring across the lava at the huge cliff face beyond, unaware that hundreds of Mudthogs were already en route to that very area. Their mission—to place a protective ring of force around the mines, and Lethavian.

"We must move quickly now, *he* knows we are here," ordered Narabius as he headed towards the lava fields.

He removed a pair of moss boots from the belt around his waist, his Shellac army did the same. By the time they reached the edge of the lava fields they were each holding a pair of dark green boots—woven from the thick, moist, moss which lined the moss caves.

"The boots will allow us to cross the lava," said Narabius as he pulled the boots on—over the top of the leather ones he already wore.

"They will only be effective for a short time. We must, therefore, move quickly if we are to be safe," he warned as he stuffed his robes into the top of his boots.

The Shellac army followed Narabius's lead as he took his first step onto the bright orange lava.

Progress over the lava was slow; and the sensation was strange—as if pulling one's feet through treacle.

Soon the whole army was nervously (but as quickly as possible) crossing the lava. The moss boots did their job well, holding back the immense heat, stopping it from burning their feet.

Narabius's brow was drenched with sweat, he felt like a pig on a spit-roast.

"KEEP MOVING.... WE ARE NEARLY THERE," he shouted, urging his army onwards.

No sooner had he spoken than the look of determination which had been etched on his face turned to one of shock; a slow-moving, single file of Mudthogs, was emerging from the salt mines.

The Mudthogs—all identical, and all carrying their feared black swords—began to encircle the entrance of the mines, at the lava's edge. Hundreds upon hundreds of them emerged from the mines -as if on a conveyor belt.

Narabius felt the immense heat from the lava beginning to penetrate his moss boots as each precious, cooling, drop of water evaporated.

To turn back, and head for the cover of the Black Forest, would now be impossible. It would result in almost certain death—his boots and those of his Shellac army were all but dry. The lava would consume their body and melt their bones. They now had no option but to carry on; to confront the Mudthogs—if they were to have any chance of survival.

"Prepare your weapons, have faith my friends," were the words Narabius planted, into the minds of his army, giving the them strength, and the encouragement, to push on. He quickly removed the bow from his shoulder and loaded one of the silver-tipped arrows. His feet were beginning to smoulder as he carefully drew back on the angel hair. He fired. The arrow shot through the air; as graceful as a swan and as fast as a bullet, striking its intended target with pinpoint accuracy. The arrow penetrated the forehead of a Mudthog, splitting it in two. It then struck another—then another -showing no sign of slowing. The arrow then sank into the wall of the salt mines and disappeared from sight. The desiccation process was instant and rendered the six Mudthogs struck by the arrow to nothing more than dust on the ground.

With a mighty leap Narabius jumped off the lava, landing on firmer, cooler, ground. He quickly picked up a black sword—dropped by a Mudthog—and began to fight for his life. He fed the minds of his fellow Shellacs, with encouragement as the battle began.

Swords and axes flew through the air, severing limbs and

splitting torsos. The size and strength of the Mudthogs horde was overpowering to the Shellac—their severed body parts reformed before their very eyes. The Shellac could not believe what they were seeing, their efforts appeared to be in vain.

Many Shellac turned and began to run back over the lava fields towards the Black Forest—they chose this way to die rather, than by the Mudthog's sword. Their painful screams filled the air as the molten lava consumed their bodies.

Narabius battled on bravely. With each accurate blow from the black sword he wielded, another Mudthog desiccated.

"THEIR WEAPONS, THEY CAN ONLY BE DESTROYED WITH THEIR OWN WEAPONS," he shouted to his army—the information hitting and registering in their brains like bolts of lightning.

Each black sword, dropped by a Mudthog, was quickly claimed by the Shellac. As the battle continued, the Mudthogs numbers began to dwindle—giving new found energy to Narabius's army.

The fighting intensified. Mudthogs began to drop like flies, as the Shellac used their heads and their hearts (as well as their extreme nimbleness) to gain control of the battlefield.

The Mudthogs had slaughtered hundreds of Shellac, but they had not bargained on the resilience of these small, determined, creatures. The table began to turn.

"VICTORY SHALL BE OURS, KEEP UP THE PRESSURE," shouted Narabius as he continued to fight like a raging bull. He relentlessly swung, sliced and stabbed at the Mudthogs—until nothing more than dust remained.

Exhausted, he dropped to his knees. His black sword crashed to the ground. They had done it—achieved the impossible. Not a single Mudthog remained standing. Narabius lifted his head to survey the area; piles of dust blew all around him—like the remains of a huge cremation. The silence was eerie. His stomach churned at the sight of so many of his Shellac army dead. Those who remained stood silently, in shock. The cold stark reality of what had happened—and what they had achieved—slowly sank in.

"We must continue," said Narabius.

"We cannot turn back. We have achieved great things, and will complete our mission, in memory of those who are no longer with us." He lowered his head, closing his eyes. They had come so far—and achieved so much. He would rather die than give up now.

Chapter 15

THE HEART OF EVILDOM

Willie placed a reassuring arm around his son as they followed Thorner along the passageway, deep within the salt mines.

"Don't worry laddie, we'll soon catch up with yer friends. I sense our mission will be over very soon—then we can all go home," he said, smiling at Cameron.

Cameron forced a smile back. "I know you're right, I just wish I was still with Finn and Erin—to help them," came his reply.

"So, tell me about Theodore—why has he changed so much? He seemed like a decent bloke when we met in the firing gallery," asked Willie with a puzzled expression.

"He was—he is—oh, I don't know. I can't quite put my finger on it," replied Cameron, desperate to find words to express himself.

"He just changed; it was after he met with Lethavian in the Black Forest. It's like... to look at him, of course he's Theodore—but, inwardly, he's not the same man. He's not as caring; quite often distant; like he's in a different place; like he wants to please Lethavian!!" Cameron's face wrinkled in displeasure, "and those eyes—they've made him ten times worse."

"Eyes?" asked Willie.

"Yes, father. Theodore replaced his sightless eyes with the evil yellow eyes that he removed from a Black Hammer," replied Cameron.

"Then Piegus is right; he *has* joined forces with his brother!" The look on Willie's face quickly turned from puzzlement... to anger.

****

Thorner came to an abrupt halt.

"He's with us; he's here, with us."

Piegus began to protest once more, but the piece of cloth (lodged firmly in his mouth) muffled his pathetic voice.

"Who's here with us?" asked Willie.

Thorner turned and smiled at the group. "Narabius; Narabius is here in the mines—he talks to me in my mind!"

"Talking? Well, what does he say?" burbled Willie in disbelief.

"He brings an army; he is here to fight alongside us," replied the Shellac warrior. "They have lost many along the way, but they are now heading to the heart of the mines—to stem the creation of Mudthogs. Then they will find The Dark Spirit and destroy him! We must go quickly; meet with him in the heart of the mines."

With that, Thorner turned and continued along the passage, the rest of the group followed him close behind.

"Not more Mudthogs! I had hoped we'd seen the last of them," sighed Cameron.

"Don't worry laddie, we know their weaknesses," smiled Willie.

****

The passageway got brighter, the deeper they went. Little pockets of light hung in the air, pushing the darkness aside, like dozens of tiny sunrises. This enabled the group to travel faster and with more ease. Because of the improved lighting, Thorner extinguished his lantern—its glow no longer required to show the way. The passageway twisted and turned, forking off in several directions. Thorner showed no hesitation in choosing which route to take. Narabius was guiding him—controlling his every action. Away in the distance, the muffled sound of activity could be heard. The sound became clearer with each step they took.

****

The heart of Lethavian's evildom hummed with activity. He had lost many of his Mudthogs during the battle with the Shellac army at the lava fields and the operation to create more had now been stepped up a pace.

Mudthog after Mudthog emerged from the bubbling pool of mud; ascending from the darkest, most evil, bowels of hell. As they emerged, they each claimed a black sword—crafted at speed from the glowing furnace. Once armed, each newly-created Mudthog took its place in the growing battalion of foot soldiers—all of whom obediently awaited instruction from their master.

****

Willie, Cameron, Lackey and their two Shellac-warrior escorts, were forced into single file as the passageway quickly narrowed.

The noise created by the production of Mudthogs, met their ears with a deafening hum. The warriors released the axes from their belts, gripping them tightly—ready for battle. Willie and Cameron each raised a black sword—recently liberated from Lethavian's defeated foot soldiers—whilst Lackey nervously clung to Willie's side.

As the group reached the throbbing heart of Mudthog production, the sight which they beheld sent a shiver—of fear and despair—down every spine. They had encountered Mudthogs on several previous occasions, but nothing on a scale like this. Tens—possibly hundreds—of Lethavian's foot soldiers stood in rows, armed and ready to do battle.

"We have little chance of victory. To destroy all of them will take no less than a miracle!" exclaimed Willie, fearing for the safety of them all.

"You forget, my friend; Narabius is also here, with *his* army. We must wait silently; await his signal," replied Hatcher.

No sooner had the words been absorbed, than Piegus's pathetic voice filled the air. He had managed to rid his mouth of the piece of cloth.

"Master, I am here. They bring an army." His voice carried well on the air, reaching the Mudthogs, who immediately turned and began to advance towards the source.

Piegus fell to the ground with a thud, as Hatcher, who had been carrying him released his grip. He lay silently, grinning to himself but unable to move as his hands and feet remained tightly-bound with rope.

"NOW YOU'VE DONE IT!" roared Willie, giving Piegus a firm kick when he saw several Mudthogs moving towards them.

Thorner and Hatcher at the front of the group stepped forward. Their bravery and sense of duty easily outweighed any feelings of fear. Although they had seen ten of their closest friends murdered by Lethavian's fire-dragon—Vandor—they would not be swayed from their mission—even if it meant they would meet a similar fate.

Willie, Cameron and Lackey quickly followed, ready to fight.

"No laddie. Take Lackey and return to the passage," instructed Willie.

"But father!" protested Cameron.

"No buts! I want you two to keep an eye on that snivelling creature who exposed us—I'll be dealing with him later," replied Willie.

Cameron reluctantly did as he was asked, returning with Lackey to the neck of the passageway.

As the Mudthogs advanced, both Shellac warriors simultaneously sent their jewel-encrusted axes spinning from their grip. The axes sliced through the air before making contact with the Mudthogs. The exquisitely-crafted weapons (just like Narabius's silver-tipped arrows) had the same effect on the Mudthogs as their own black swords. The targets were instantly desiccated. The axes flew through the air at speed, slicing through several Mudthogs before circling around, like boomerangs, to head back to their owners. They sliced through several more Mudthogs on their return journey before safely finding their way back into the hands of the Shellac warriors.

"Well I never—six apiece," shouted Willie excitedly. "Maybe this battle won't be all that one-sided after all!"

More Mudthogs were now deployed, closing in from all directions. Already, twelve more had emerged from the bubbling pool of mud, each one armed and ready to fight. They were replacements for the twelve destroyed moments before by the Shellac warriors.

Thorner and Hatcher continued to use their axes, desiccating several Mudthogs each with every throw they made. As the battle continued, the sheer number of Mudthogs advancing upon them began to overpower the brave trio.

Willie defended himself as a lethal black sword rained down upon him. He swung with all his might, firmly holding his sword with both hands. The blow was deflected and, with a forceful thrust, Willie sank his blade deep into the belly of the Mudthog. No effort was required to withdraw the weapon as the desiccation process came instantly, reducing the foot soldier to mere dust at Willie's feet.

He continued to fight, furiously swinging, stabbing and slicing with his sword; the Mudthogs' attack showed no sign of abating.

The accuracy of Willie's blows was pretty much irrelevant; as long as his blade made firm contact with its target, the Mudthogs solidified, then crumbled!

The Shellac warriors continued to battle, wielding their axes with force, but, as more Mudthogs closed in, the force with which the weapons left their grip decreased.

As an axe span furiously towards its target, it met with the cold black metal of a Mudthogs sword. The axe deflected from its course, spiralled out of control and crashed into the wall of the cavern before hitting the ground.

Unarmed Thorner stood bravely defiant, as a Mudthog sank its lethal weapon into his chest.

The warrior's face contorted in agony, but he did not cry out. The brave manner in which he accepted his death made his friends proud. He stood silent and strong as his life drained away. The Mudthog twisted its sword before withdrawing it from its victim and allowing Thorner's lifeless body to slump to the ground.

Willie span round, angered by the tragedy of what he had just witnessed. He swung his sword, severing the head clean off the Mudthog's shoulders.

Hatcher continued to battle alongside Willie—but their efforts appeared futile. The bubbling pool of mud continued to produce Mudthog after Mudthog, replacing each and every fallen one just as quickly as they fell. Hatcher continued to defend both himself and Willie; dust from the defeated Mudthogs filled the air, nipping at his eyes and sending tears rolling down his cheeks. He held his axe firmly, slicing it into any approaching Mudthog.

The Warrior suddenly froze to the ground where he stood; his deadly axe was still firmly in his grip, but he was as still as a statue. He felt a deep, burning pain—like a red-hot poker—between his shoulder blades. His hearing became muffled, his vision blurred. The sound of his slowing heartbeat filled his head. Disorientated and exhausted, he dropped to his knees as a Mudthog withdrew its blade from his back. A warm, calming, feeling flushed through his body and, like a candle being starved of oxygen, his life faded away, Hatcher was gone!

****

Cameron screwed his eyes tightly shut; fists clenched, he dropped to his knees and beat the ground in despair. The sight of a life being extinguished pained him to the heart. Within a split second he lifted his head and snapped his eyes open—only to find he was faced with another group of advancing Mudthogs and that only he, Lackey and his father now remained.

Willie—now surrounded by Mudthogs—frantically swung, stabbed and sliced with his sword. He was being attacked from every direction.

Cameron did not hesitate for one second. He ran from the relative safety of the passageway, leaving Lackey to watch over Piegus. He threw himself at the advancing Mudthogs, his black sword held firmly. He sliced, stabbed and thrusted the blade as he went. Mudthogs crumbled at his side, having been taken completely by surprise.

Willie continued to defend himself in all directions, but his energy was quickly sapping away due to his sustained efforts. The sight of Cameron rushing to his defence spurred him on but, as his blade smashed into that of a Mudthog's sword, it was sent reeling from his grip. The blade severed the heads clean from two more Mudthogs before crashing to the ground, out of his reach. Willie now stood unarmed. Time appeared to slow as he tracked the path of the Mudthog's weapon, inch by inch, as it approached him. With no way of defending himself, he took one final glance at his son. Cameron continued to fight with all his strength. Willie smiled to himself; even in the face of death, the love and pride he felt for his son filled his heart. Fixing his gaze back to the advancing blade, he lifted his hands and covered his face, hoping that his death would be instant.

Cameron frantically tried to reach his father's side, but he was overpowered by the constant onslaught from Lethavian's slimy foot soldiers. He felt lost; completely helpless. Suddenly he was distracted; something caught his eye as it flew at speed, past him and towards Willie.

****

The angel hair felt so delicate as Narabius released it from between his thumb and forefinger, sending a silver-tipped arrow from his bow. The arrow only narrowly missed Cameron as it passed by him. It hit its target with force, like an express train thundering into a tunnel. The arrow penetrated the head of the Mudthog, whose blade was now just inches away from Willie. The desiccation came instantly. Just as Willie braced himself, ready to pass over into the afterlife, the sound of the Mudthog's lethal black sword crashing to the ground, reached his ears. The sound flushed into his eardrums, hitting his brain, like sweet liquid amber. He quickly dropped to his knees, grabbed the sword and swung it with all his strength. The cold blade severed the legs from any Mudthog within striking distance; he was showered with dust as they crumbled to the ground.

Willie opened his eyes and glanced upwards. His attention was drawn to the small platform from which Piegus had previously addressed Lethavian's army. As he strained to focus he was met by the face of Narabius, smiling down at him.

Narabius's Shellac army entered the heart of the evildom from all directions, charging towards the Mudthogs with vigour. They were so nimble that they were able to dodge the blades of the Mudthog, whose numbers soon began to decrease—and at a faster rate than they could be produced from the bubbling womb of mud.

Cameron had now reached his father's side. Exhausted they looked at one another, each raising a smile.

"Lucky white heather!" remarked Willie with a wink of his eye, before slicing the head clean from the shoulders of another Mudthog.

As the battle continued, the Shellac army slowly began to take control of the situation. They used the black swords—originally crafted for their own downfall, to destroy Lethavian's army of Mudthogs.

Realisation of their victory came to the remaining Shellac as the final Mudthog hit the ground. Anxiety turned to relief, which they could not contain—like a butterfly breaking free of its chrysalis. An almighty cheer filled the air.

Piles of dust and black swords littered the ground. The dust appeared to smoulder as it was shifted by the breeze which blew through the mines, along the many passageways, drawn from the air outside.

Willie dropped his sword and glanced upwards, to where Narabius stood. "You took yer time wee man!, I thought I was gonnae have to defeat these lumps of mud single-handed!"

Narabius smiled down. "Sorry Willie, I didn't mean to spoil your fun," came his reply.

Willie flung his arms around Cameron, his joy, plainly obvious.

"I'll always remember the bravery you showed today—a true McDougal ye certainly are," he said, beaming at his son.

The bubbling mud continued to produce Mudthog after Mudthog; but, as they emerged, the Shellac army took great pleasure in relieving them of their heads. They took the opportunity for a spot of target practice; the more accurate the blow—the more points scored.

Narabius joined Willie at ground level. "You have done well my large friend; achieving the almost unachievable. I am just sorry my decision to join you came so late in the day," he said, forcing a frustrated smile.

"Late in the day! I would say yer timing could nae have bin better," replied Willie. "You saved ma life—for that I shall always be grateful to ye."

****

Lackey emerged from the passageway, dragging Piegus with him—kicking and screaming.

"My master will destroy you, he will be angered by your actions! Release me now and I shall plead with him to spare your life," he snivelled.

Piegus felt a hand—the size of a shovel—as it grabbed him by the scruff of the neck and lift him clean off the ground.

"Release me now," he protested, just as Willie dropped the spineless wretch at Narabius's feet.

"One of yours, I believe," boomed the orange-haired giant.

"No Willie; he may be of Shellac descent, but he is no longer one of ours," replied Narabius.

"Then he belongs with the Mudthogs; let them decide his fate!" exclaimed Willie. He grabbed Piegus once more by the scruff of the neck and, lifting him aloft, carried him to the edge of the bubbling mud pool.

"Let me go; join with us—secure your future," demanded Piegus.

"Unbelievable! Even in the face of death, your arrogance overflows!" scowled Willie. "You want me to let you go do yer? Well, I suppose I *could* manage that." Obligingly, Willie released his grip. Piegus hit the mud with a glug. Its viscosity held him briefly, while he flapped his arms and legs. The mud then slowly sucked him in, dragging him down; his protest futile, he disappeared from sight.

The mud pool momentarily calmed, but it wasn't long before a flurry of new activity began. The surface began to bubble, furiously, spitting globules of phlegm-like particles in all directions. A single column of mud then erupted from its bowels and, like a geyser blowing its load, leapt at least thirty feet skyward. The torrent of erupting mud soon began to subside; after only a few minutes it fell silent; not a single bubble emerged from the surface. The entire pool solidified, hardening like stone. The solidified mud acted as a huge bung and, like a cork holding its contents firmly in a bottle, stemmed the rise of any more Mudthogs.

"Let's see yer master save yer now!" exclaimed Willie with a smile. He turned his back on the freshly-sealed mud pool and walked over to Narabius.

"The day Piegus turned his back on his own kind was the day he sealed his fate! A lesson, I believe, to us all," said Narabius with a heavy heart.

His sadness soon lifted, when the sound of his army celebrating their success, reached his eardrums.

The deceased Shellac were laid with great care at one side of the cavern, where respect was then duly paid. Narabius stood silently, remembering those who had given their lives so unselfishly.

The breeze which blew through the evildom turned icy cold all of a sudden. Narabius felt the presence of someone—or something—observing them. He glanced up at the spot from which he had fired the arrow that had saved Willie's life. His eyes landed on the figure of a man. The man was dressed entirely in black; his head and face—shrouded by a cloth. Perched on the man's left shoulder was a Black Hammer, its piercing yellow eyes scanned the area. The horrors of the recent battle slipped into near obscurity. Silence fell like a wet blanket, smothering the proceedings.

"Lethavian! I wondered when we would finally meet," said Narabius in a firm manner. "Look around us, no foot soldiers to protect you now!"

Lethavian did not speak. He raised an arm, exposing a grey, bony, hand. He slowly uncurled a finger and pointed it at Willie.

"Me is it? Yer want me? Well come on then—*I'll* nae run from ye," boomed Willie, slightly unnerved by the sight of The Dark Spirit. Lethavian continued to stand, silently. He clicked his fingers, as if to demonstrate the ease with which he alone would determine who would live and who would die. He then turned and walked back into the darkness of the mines.

The air temperature soon returned to its original state and the cavern started to hum, once more, with conversation.

"So that's who we're all trembling aboot! A man that dare not even show us his face!" said Willie, insulted and angered by Lethavian's arrogance—even in defeat.

"He'll have to do more than click his fingers to rid this place of me!"

"Save your energy Willie, you shall need every drop of it—and more, I feel, all too soon," advised Narabius.

"So, at last, I meet with your son Cameron. I had heard of it—but now I have seen your bravery with my own eyes. I am indeed honoured to be joining you."

Cameron took hold of Narabius's outstretched hand. "The pleasure is all mine; and, for saving my father's life, *I* am at *your* service," he replied.

"Then we will continue together, Cameron. I believe you have friends that you wish to be reunited with?" said a smiling Narabius. Cameron nodded in response, focusing his thoughts on Erin and Finn.

"Gather your weapons, the final push must come now! He has been weakened. You have done well my friends," instructed Narabius.

His army quickly obeyed his words. Within minutes they were again on the march, Narabius leading, their goal—to find Lethavian.

Chapter 16

RAVENHALL

"Don't trust him, he isn't who he says he is!" whispered Cameron to Finn and Erin, as they walked briskly to keep up with Theodore.

"How do you know? I know he's been acting a bit strange, but how do you *truly* know?" pressed Finn, intrigued by Cameron's suggestion.

"If I told you, you wouldn't believe me, just trust me for now! When the time is right, I'll expose the truth," replied Cameron.

Erin looked bewildered.

"Just act as normal as possible—as if nothing has changed." Cameron smiled and gave a reassuring wink.

Theodore led the group through the maze of twisting passageways, so instinctively, it seemed he either had a sixth sense, or more sinisterly, he knew the way.

Erin froze to the spot. Again she sensed a thousand eyes burning into her back. Her body tingled, as if an electric current was surging through her. This time the feeling was more intense than the sensation she had experienced before; she found herself unable to move or speak.

The eerie sound of a muffled voice permeated her thoughts.

'Save our souls.'

The words were repeated—over and over again—until, as quickly as the feeling had come over her, it lifted and was gone.

Erin hurried to catch up with the group, but remained silent about her experience.

"Theodore, are you sure you know where you're going?" asked

Finn.

"Oh yes my child, I have followed this path many times—in my mind of course," came his reply, from behind a wry smile. "It is not far now, soon we shall meet with my master... er, I mean, my brother," he sniggered.

The temperature in the passage had plummeted to such an extent that the warm, moist breath expelled by the three friends left their mouths like puffs of smoke—lingering a while, before being carried away in the breeze.

"Theodore, wait a minute. What's happening to the temperature? It's as if we're standing in a freezer!" asked Erin

Theodore stopped and turned to the group. "We are here! We have reached Lethavian's quarters—he never was one for warmth!" Theodore's eyes sparkled as he spoke, "come now, the entrance is just ahead."

In the distance, somewhere out of view, the faint sound of wings—flapping—could be heard. The sound slowly increased, both in speed and volume—like a beating drum, gathering pace to the final crescendo.

"Keep calm, I believe we are about to be joined by some Black Hammers, do not be afraid," urged Cameron.

"Did you notice the absence of breath escaping from Theodore's mouth when he spoke? No vapour hanging in the air," said Finn raising an eyebrow.

Erin gulped hard. "Then Cameron is right, he's not who he pretends to be."

Cameron took hold of Erin's hand. "Don't worry, I shall look out for all of us."

The sound of the wings, beating the air, was now the only sound to be heard. The noise intensified. Then they began to notice, here and there, the appearance of evil, yellow eyes, peering at them from the darkness.

"Cover yourselves," instructed Cameron, as hundreds of birds passed overhead. They swarmed like bees, showing no sign of slowing as they raced through the passageway. Erin, Finn and Cameron huddled on the ground, heads covered, fearing attack. After several minutes the sound of the birds abated. They had passed over without incident—much to their relief.

The three friends lifted their heads. One by one their gazes landed upon Theodore. He was standing just in front of them, next to a large, solid-looking black door. The door was open. Beyond it could be seen the Black Hammers, perching everywhere possible.

"Welcome to Ravenhall," announced Theodore, beckoning the

three friends to follow him inside.

Tentatively, Cameron, Finn and Erin, rose to their feet and stepped through the doorway.

They found themselves in a large and peculiar-looking room. It had several doors leading off it and sported a minstrel gallery at one end.

The walls were made of black marble, they were aged and rugged. There was little in the way of furniture, except for a large, throne-like, chair which was fixed to a slightly-raised platform in the centre of the room. It was constructed from the same black marble as the walls. The room was dimly lit by a dozen or so flames, positioned around the room. They flickered, suspended by nothing but the air itself, there certainly were no candles supporting them. The room was named after its grandiose appearance and, of course, the Black Hammers similarity to Ravens.

Erin jumped with fright. The large door, through which they had just entered, had slammed shut behind them. Such was the force with which the door had slammed, it caused the Black Hammers to stir; squawking, they leapt from their perches and filled the air with ear-splitting shrieks.

Erin put her hands over her ears to protect them from the racket. The Black Hammers slowly settled themselves once more and the noise gradually decreased.

Theodore stood laughing at the three friends, all of whom looked somewhat overwhelmed. He then turned, in the centre of the hall, to face the throne.

"Master, I have returned with the spoils you requested," he grovelled, dropping to his knees.

"Theodore! What are you doing?" demanded Erin, confused by his actions.

Theodore turned to face the three friends but gave no reply; his evil, yellow, eyes seemed more menacing than ever. After a few moments he turned back towards the throne, stretched out his arms and laid his hands on its legs.

The ground began to rumble, as if something deep in the earth was stirring. The rumbling intensified, causing the three friends to grab hold of each other to steady themselves.

"WHAT'S HAPPENING, CAMERON?" screamed Erin in fear.

Before he could answer, a black mist began to billow around the throne. The mist coiled, spinning furiously—like a tornado—hell-bent on destruction. Then, slowly, it began to change shape, eventually taking on a human form.

Finn's eyeballs almost bulged out of their sockets, in awe

of what he was seeing. The human form became clearer until, suddenly, the rumbling stopped and silence descended once more. The three friends could do nothing but stare at Lethavian, who now sat before them.

****

As Narabius led his army—accompanied by Willie, Cameron and Lackey—through the passageway, the ground beneath them moved. Like a mini earthquake, from deep within the earth's core, it sent a shockwave to the surface. The walls of the passage began to crumble and the ground began to fold. Many of the Shellac army were thrown from their feet by the sheer force of the tremors. The whole thing was over in mere seconds—almost as if it had never happened.

"What was that?" asked Cameron, picking himself up from the ground.

"I can only assume that it was our host! We must move, quickly, before it is too late," replied Narabius.

****

Erin, Finn and Cameron, stood in silence as Lethavian stirred. Slowly, he lifted his head and drew back his shroud. His pale complexion and twisted features did his reputation justice! *His* evil, yellow, eyes were more terrifying than those of any of his Black Hammers. Around his neck hung the Purple Crystal. He gripped the bulbous ends at the arms of his throne, pushing himself to his feet. He stood silently for a moment, as if he was a speaker on a dais, waiting to address his audience.

He parted his lips, exposing an array of decayed and discoloured teeth.

"At last we meet! I am finally face to face with the three intrepid fools who believe they are here to destroy me!"

Lethavian made a fist with one hand and hammered it into the palm of his open hand as he spoke.

"Well—here I am! Destroy me, if you really think you are able."

He flung his arms open, at the same time lifting his eyes to the ceiling. He stood motionless, as if nailed to a cross, before focusing his eyes back on the three friends.

"Well you won't get a better offer," he said, releasing a most hideous laugh.

The hundreds of Black Hammers perched in the hall took flight, the sound of their beating wings amplifying the laughter.

Cameron could not hold himself back any longer. He grabbed

the jewel-encrusted axe from Finn (the one reclaimed from Vandor's nest) and lunged at his tormentor.

Lethavian remained nonchalant as Theodore stepped in, to protect his brother. Wielding a black sword, he deflected Cameron's blow with ease and sent him sprawling across the floor. The Black Hammers swarmed above them, as if excited by the battle below. Cameron managed to right himself, just as Theodore's sword was about to crash down upon him. The handle of his axe took the brunt of the blow, the force of which sent Cameron reeling once more.

Finn took hold of Erin, pulling her away from the battle zone and towards the doorway of the hall. The Black Hammers quickly descended upon them, blocking their movement and trapping them in a corner.

Theodore's blade plummeted towards Cameron, who lay—somewhat dazed—on the ground. Suddenly, realising his impending doom, he rolled to one side, swinging his axe at Theodore's legs. The axe narrowly missed its target, but sent Theodore jumping to safety.

Cameron took a breath, composing himself before again swinging wildly with his axe at Theodore. The block came all too swiftly and, once again, his attack was deflected from its target. Theodore sliced his blade at Cameron, only slightly catching his cheek with its tip. The faintest trickle of blood appeared on his face as the skin split open.

****

Erin shut her eyes tightly as she screamed in fear. A burning pain filled her head as the face of Theodore appeared in her mind.

'Fear not, child. A book should never be judged by its cover!' he whispered to her, before vacating her mind. She quickly flicked her eyes wide open and was greeted by the sight of Cameron blocking yet another blow. And then—sinking his axe into Theodore's skull!

The desiccation was swift. Theodore crumbled to dust and, in seconds, he was no more.

Erin, now totally confused, followed Cameron's movements, her brain, muddled. Time appeared to slow as she watched Cameron turn to face the black, solid, doorway, through which they had entered the hall. He sent his axe spinning from his grip. The axe—to Erin's eyes at least—moved slowly, slicing its way through the air like the second hand of a watch, so steady was the momentum. The axe flew through the mass of Black Hammers, severing heads and wings as it went. Finally it smashed into the bolt on the door, breaking it easily, as if it was made of glass.

As time returned to its more normal state, Erin watched the door to Ravenhall burst open, as Narabius charged in—bringing his army with him.

The Black Hammers attacked, digging their claws into delicate, Shellac, skin; but the attack was too little, too late and the Shellac had soon restored control to the hall.

Lethavian remained on the platform which housed his throne. Cameron raised one hand, unleashing a magical force which rendered him statue-like.

Willie entered the hall, confused by the sight which greeted him. By his side stood his son—Cameron—but Cameron also, stood, in the hall, controlling Lethavian. He stared- dumbfounded—watching, as the Cameron who had battled hard with Theodore, with blood running down his cheek, began to change in appearance. Through the ability of metamorphosis he changed into, non other than, the *real* Theodore Ping!!

Narabius loaded his bow with his last-remaining silver-tipped arrow, drew back on the angel hair and fired it at Lethavian. The arrow struck the necklace that had secured the Purple Crystal to its keeper since it was stolen from Theodore many years ago. The arrow split the chain, parting Lethavian from the one thing that had allowed him the power to pursue his desire: it then sank itself deep into his chest.

Lethavian released an agonising cry before reducing to a dense, black, mist.

The temperature in the hall instantly increased and, as the black mist cleared, nothing remained of Lethavian. Nothing, that was, except the Purple Crystal, which lay glowing on the ground where it had fallen.

Theodore hurried to reclaim it. As soon as he clasped his hands firmly around it, the crystal glowed brighter than he had ever known. With a mixture of emotions, he gently kissed the crystal before securing it safely under his cassock.

Willie felt a warm, pleasing, sensation emanate from his pocket. He placed his hand inside and withdrew the smooth white stone that had been entrusted to him in the Ocean of evil, the same one that had saved him from the Shadow Demons in the Black Forest. He held the stone aloft; it glowed like a beacon.

"Place the stone on the marble seat," instructed Theodore, pointing at Lethavian's throne.

Willie did as he was asked, then quickly stepped back when the stone began to pulsate with activity, turning an array of different colours. It then cracked open—like an egg, giving life to whatever had grown inside it. The hall became a hive of activity, as thousands of shafts of light extruded from the stone, dancing and flying in every direction.

Erin was unable to move. The thousands of eyes that had made their presence felt to her on many previous occasions were here again! This time, however, the eyes belonged to a multitude of smiling faces; the smiling faces of the countless souls claimed by Lethavian had finally been released from their incarceration: released to finally roam freely and to pass over to the afterlife.

****

"THEODORE! WE'VE DONE IT," screamed Erin excitedly, as she flung her arms around him.

"Yes child, our quest is over," he replied, a grin spreading, like treacle, on his face.

"I thought you were dead. How did you change like that? Where did you come from?" asked Finn, desperate for answers.

"It's a long story," he replied, still grinning with satisfaction.

"Lethavian tried to take me captive in the Black Forest when he called me to him. Fortunately I was able to escape. I slipped off his horse, still in the sack which he had placed me in."

"*That's* what he was carrying! We saw him riding over the lake; *You* were in his sack?" burbled Cameron.

"Yes child, that was me. Luckily I managed to free myself before I drowned; I presume that's what Lethavian thought had happened to me."

"Then what? How did you get here?" urged Erin.

"That was the easy part—I just followed you."

"Followed us, how? You can't see!" replied Finn.

Theodore started to chuckle. "I *had* no sight; now, however, I can see!—Lethavian's parting gift in the Black Forest, he thought he could buy my cooperation," he answered, rapidly blinking his eyelids excitedly—like a child playing with a new toy.

"I was aware that Lethavian had sent you my replacement—not such a handsome beast as myself, I must say!" he continued.

"Once in the salt mine, I waited for my chance. Fortunately, when the Mudthog tried to kill you, Cameron, your father was there to save you. I took that opportunity to use a little trick, one that I hadn't used in a long time."

"You turned yourself into me," said Cameron.

"Exactly! Metamorphosis used to be my favourite party trick. You witnessed the rest—and here we are!"

The three friends simultaneously flung their arms around Theodore, words failing them.

****

As the tired—but happily victorious, group stepped out of the salt mines, the sight that greeted them was like nothing they had seen before. The orange glow of the lava fields had gone, having been replaced by an expanse of solid rock. The dark moon was no more; in its place shone a large, warming, sun. The Black Forest was now green; and new life sprouted everywhere. The gentle sound of birds, singing happily, hung in the air.

****

The Shellac who had given their lives were gathered, to be returned as promised to their homeland.

The cost of ridding the world of The Dark Spirit had been immense, but the benefits would be even greater.

The Purple Crystal was entrusted to Narabius for safe keeping, to allow the Shellac opportunity to rebuild their community with no fear of reprisal.

Theodore was offered a home with Narabius, which he accepted.

"I'll stay a while, a bit of respite will do me the world of good; and the water of life, well, I'll be drinking gallons of the stuff," he said gleefully.

Lackey decided to remain with Willie—the one (and only) true friend he had ever known.

After some emotional farewells, Willie, Lackey, Finn, Erin and Cameron, left for home.

The day was just breaking; a bright yellow sun warmed the air as the lodge came into sight.

"Home at last! I don't intend going anywhere, ever again! Well, at least for a few weeks," grinned Willie.

"Come on you two, we must get yer back to Mrs Mac's; yer parents must be worried sick!"

Finn and Erin turned to Cameron. "Farewell Cameron—and thank you for everything!" said Finn.

"Keep in touch, please!" pleaded Erin.

"Try and stop me, I'll start writing today," smiled Cameron.

"Come on then, let's get ye back," urged Willie as he turned, heading towards the village.

As they walked into the little hamlet of Ping, life was just stirring. The butcher was busy filling his window, and the most mouth-watering aroma of freshly-baked bread wafted from the baker's shop.

"Ah, there you both are!" said Mr Blackwell, as Finn and Erin approached the Eagle View guest house.

"I hoped you'd be back early, I thought we'd have a drive up to Tartan Sands," he suggested.

"And you must be Mr McDougal, I do hope they behaved themselves for you last night?" Mr Blackwell offered Willie his outstretched hand.

"A finer couple of bairns ye could nae meet," replied Willie.

Goodbyes, and addresses, were exchanged before Finn and Erin jumped into their father's car. They were soon joined by Mrs Blackwell and, with a turn of a key, they were off.

As the car trundled out of the sleepy little village, the evil, yellow, eye of a solitary Black Hammer caught their attention.

"Look," said Finn pointing at the raven-like creature.

"It couldn't be, could it?"

www.ingramcontent.com/pod-product-compliance
Ingram Content Group UK Ltd.
Pitfield, Milton Keynes, MK11 3LW, UK
UKHW041943190726
13854UKWH00004B/1771